"Hands o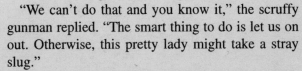

Fargo cocked the Colt. "Not one twitch or you're dead."

The men holding Flora froze. One of them snickered. "Well, ain't this cozy? Did the widow-lady make you feel right to home?"

"Shuck those gunbelts," Fargo instructed them.

"We can't do that and you know it," the scruffy gunman replied. "The smart thing to do is let us on out. Otherwise, this pretty lady might take a stray slug."

The man had a point. Even if Fargo put a bullet into each of them, Flora might get hurt. The cutthroat holding Flora let go and backpedaled. The third man was slow to leave. It didn't go unnoticed.

"Don't be a jackass, Mull," the scruffy one said. "He's got us dead to rights."

"I don't back down for no one," Mull said gruffly.

Fargo sidled to the right for a clear shot. Flora caught his eye and bobbed her chin at the floor. Before he could shake his head, she flung herself out of harm's way.

"Now, Skye! Now!"

All three gunmen stabbed for their six-guns, and Fargo fired away. . . .

THE
TRAILSMAN
#220

MONTANA
GUN SHARPS

by

Jon Sharpe

A SIGNET BOOK

SIGNET
Published by New American Library, a division of
Penguin Putnam Inc., 375 Hudson Street,
New York, New York 10014, U.S.A.
Penguin Books Ltd, 27 Wrights Lane,
London W8 5TZ, England
Penguin Books Australia Ltd,
Ringwood, Victoria, Australia
Penguin Books Canada Ltd, 10 Alcorn Avenue,
Toronto, Ontario, Canada M4V 3B2
Penguin Books (N.Z.) Ltd, 182–190 Wairau Road,
Auckland 10, New Zealand

Penguin Books Ltd, Registered Offices:
Harmondsworth, Middlesex, England

First published by Signet, an imprint of New American Library,
a division of Penguin Putnam Inc.

First Printing, February 2000
10 9 8 7 6 5 4 3 2 1

The first chapter of this book originally appeared in *Arizona Silver Strike*,
the two hundred nineteenth volume in this series.

 REGISTERED TRADEMARK—MARCA REGISTRADA

Printed in the United States of America

PUBLISHER'S NOTE
This is a work of fiction. Names, characters, places and incidents are either the
product of the author's imagination or are used fictitiously, and any resemblance to
actual persons, living or dead, business establishments, events, or locales is entirely
coincidental.

The Trailsman

Beginnings . . . they bend the tree and they mark the man. Skye Fargo was born when he was eighteen. Terror was his midwife, vengeance his first cry. Killing spawned Skye Fargo, ruthless, cold-blooded murder. Out of the acrid smoke of gunpowder still hanging in the air, he rose, cried out a promise never forgotten.

The Trailsman they began to call him all across the West: searcher, scout, hunter, the man who could see where others only looked, his skills for hire but not his soul, the man who lived each day to the fullest, yet trailed each tomorrow. Skye Fargo, the Trailsman, and the seeker who could take the wildness of a land and the wanting of a woman and make them his own.

Montana, 1860—
where desperate men ply their trade
with quick triggers, and the word
of one man stands as law
in a lawless frontier. . . .

1

The big man in buckskins reined up beside a crude wooden sign. His piercing lake blue eyes rose to the fork just ahead and the rutted excuse for a road that wound to the north, then he glanced down again at the sign. "Silver Flats," he read aloud to his Ovaro. "Two miles."

Skye Fargo had never heard of the place, which wasn't unusual. Based on its name, he guessed it must be a boom town, and boom towns were like weeds these days. They sprang up wherever a strike was claimed, saw their day in the sun, and withered as soon as the ore played out. Ordinarily he would have passed Silver Flats by without a second thought, but he had been on the trail for weeks and his stallion could use a day or two of rest. So, for that matter, could he.

In no great hurry, Fargo reined northward, holding to a walk. The morning sun was warm on his back and the lush forest on either side was alive with the chirping of birds and the occasional chittering of squirrels. All seemed peaceful, yet Fargo never let down his guard. He had no hankering to go to an early grave, and staying alert was the key to staying alive—in the wilds or close to civilization.

Before long, Fargo detected the acrid odor of smoke. His hand strayed to the butt of the Colt on his hip as he straightened in the saddle. After another hundred yards, he heard voices. Coming around a bend, he saw three men hunkered around a fire in a crescent-shaped clearing on the left. Fargo's wariness flared, tightening his gut. The three had the unmistakable stamp of hardcases. It showed in their flinty faces, in their low-slung revolvers, and in their coiled postures. They spotted him right away and all three rose, their hands hanging near their hardware.

Fargo intended to ride on by. Who they were and what they were up to was of no concern to him. All he was interested in was a cozy bed in a warm hotel room. After he treated himself to a few whiskeys, of course, and maybe an evening of cards. Not to mention the willing company of a fallen dove. But as he neared the clearing, the three curly wolves edged to the side of the road.

The shortest, a runt with a shock of red hair and cheeks dotted with large freckles, swaggered into the road, barring the pinto's way. He wore a big Remington and carried himself like a grown man, but Fargo guessed he couldn't be more than sixteen or seventeen years old, if that. Pushing his narrow-brimmed hat back on his head, he grinned good-naturedly. His tone held a different edge entirely. "Hold up there, stranger. We'd like a few words with you. Where might you be headed?"

Fargo drew rein. He supposed he could be civil, but the pup's arrogance was grating. "None of your damn business."

The kid was smarter than he appeared. He didn't get mad or toss an insult back. Instead, his grin widened. "There's no call to get uppity, mister. I'm Billy Pardee. Maybe you've heard of me?"

"Can't say that I have." Fargo watched the other two closely. One was tall and lanky with eyes as cold as ice. The other was average in every respect except for a jagged scar down his left cheek. Neither showed any interest in unlimbering their irons, but Fargo wasn't taking anything for granted.

"Well, down in the Staked Plain country, folks sure know me," Pardee said, sounding disappointed. "I've blown out the wicks of more hombres than I can count."

Fargo's opinion of the upstart fell even more. Only a

jackass would brag about killing. "You're a long way from Texas."

Pardee chuckled. "It got a little too warm for comfort, if you savvy my meanin'. So my friends and me lit a shuck. Been ridin' the high lines ever since, blowin' wherever the winds take us."

In other words, Fargo translated, the law was after them, probably because of the runt's itchy trigger finger.

"You have the look of a man who knows a teat from a tit," Pardee went on. "I reckon you must know these parts pretty well. We'd be obliged if you'd tell us how we can find Luther Teller."

"Don't know the man," Fargo said, lifting the reins. "I'm as new to this neck of the woods as you are." He'd made it plain he wanted to ride on but the runt didn't move from in front of the Ovaro.

"We heard tell he's lookin' for gents who are handy in a shootin' scrape," the young gunman mentioned.

"And you figure to hire on," Fargo guessed.

"Why not? It's what I do best, so why not get paid for blowing windows in a few skulls? A man has to make a livin', doesn't he?"

"Ask me again when you *are* a man," Fargo rejoined. He didn't know what made him say it. He wasn't looking for trouble. But he had an overwhelming urge to put this runt in his place.

Billy Pardee stiffened, his grin fading. "Mister, you shouldn't go around insultin' people. Not unless you're partial to a lead diet."

"Should I tremble in fear now or later?"

The young gun shark glared, his arm hooked to claw at his six-shooter. "I don't eat crow for anyone, ever. You'll apologize . . . or else."

It was then that the man with the scar came to life. Stepping quickly to Pardee's side, he placed a restraining hand on his wrist. "We don't want no trouble, Billy remember? We don't want to draw any attention to ourselves."

Pardee wrenched the man's hand off his arm. "Who's to know, Decker?"

"Keller might hear of it and we'll be out of a job," Decker said. "Remember, the word was to drift quietlike."

"He's right," said the tall drink of water with icy eyes.

Pardee continued to scowl at Fargo, his hand quivering above his revolver. Fargo was certain the Texan would slap leather, but again Pardee surprised him by lowering his arm and shrugging.

"Looks like I'm outvoted, stranger. We'll meet again, though. I'll make a point of it. And next time I won't sheathe my claws."

Fargo nudged the stallion with his knees. It moved forward so quickly that the freckle-faced gunman had to bound out of the way or be bowled over. Swiveling in the saddle, Fargo didn't take his eyes off the three gunmen until another bend hid them. Even then, he continued to check over his shoulder. Pardee didn't strike him as the sort who cared overly much whether he shot someone in the front or in the back. Only after a mile without incident did Fargo feel safe.

The forest ended at a broad strip of grassy flatland situated at the base of the Anaconda Range. The stark, rugged Rocky Mountains, covered with fir, pine, and spruce, was a region scarcely explored let alone settled, home to grizzlies without number and hostiles without mercy. Several peaks glistened with caps of pristine snow.

But it was the town of Silver Flats at their base that interested Fargo most. It was bigger than he expected, with thirty to forty buildings, some no more than planks thrown together with high false fronts. As a boom town, it should have been bustling with activity but he only saw a handful of people abroad. Rather dull and drab, Fargo thought.

Fargo entered the wide main street, passing a stable, a general store, a butcher's, an inn named Etta's Lodgings, and a tack shop. Halting at a hitch rail in front of the town's saloon, he dismounted. A middle-aged woman was walking by and he touched the brim of his hat to her. She ignored him. Gazing up and down the street, he realized that all the other people out and about were women as well. There wasn't a man in sight.

Puzzled, Fargo removed his hat and used it to slap some of the dust from his buckskins. Then, licking his lips in anticipation, he ambled into the saloon and over to the bar. It was still early but Fargo expected to find at least a few thirsty souls present. Yet no one else was there. The saloon was empty save for a crusty old bartender who was polishing glasses with an air of total boredom.

"Where is everyone?" Fargo inquired.

The barkeep looked up. "Thunderation! I didn't hear you come in!" Beaming like a politician on the stump, he wiped his hands on his apron and beckoned. "Don't be shy, friend. Come on over. I haven't had a paying customer in so long, I'm about ready to start talking to myself."

His puzzlement growing, Fargo strolled to the counter. "How can that be in a town this size? Don't tell me the temperance movement has spread this far?"

"Hell, I wish that was all it was." The bartender thrust out a calloused hand. "Irish Mike is my handle. I've been pouring coffin varnish for more years than I care to recollect. Name your poison."

Fargo requested whiskey. A dog barked outside, the lone sound emphasizing how dead quiet the town was. By rights, Silver Flats should be filled with constant racket. "Has the silver played out? Most everyone pull up stakes and leave?" Fargo wondered.

"Oh, not hardly, boyo," Irish Mike said, pouring three fingers' worth into a shot glass. "You're new to these parts or you'd know that most of the men are up at the mine. The Silverlode, it's called."

"When do they get back? Sunset?"

"Lordy, I wish." Irish Mike treated himself to a glass. "No, they go up on Monday morning and don't return until Friday evening. That alone is bad enough. I have practi-

5

cally no customers all week and then more than I can handle over the weekend. But in the past two months it's gotten a lot worse. Men can't buy drinks with money they don't have."

Fargo raised the glass to his lips. Savoring a slow sip, he felt the welcome burning sensation spread down his throat into the pit of his stomach. "How's that again?"

"They haven't been paid. The owner is expecting money at any time. But between you and me, if it doesn't get here soon those miners are likely to walk off the job. Then this town will dry up and blow away with the wind."

The news was interesting but of no personal importance to Fargo. He polished off the first glass and gestured for another. In a way he was glad he had the place all to himself. He'd spend a quiet day or two to give the stallion time to rest up, then continue on to Butte.

"I came here thinking to make money hand over fist," Irish Mike was saying, "and for a while I did. So I reckon I shouldn't complain just because George Prescott has had a run of powerful bad luck."

"Who?"

"Prescott. The owner of the Silverlode Mine. Or, rather, the manager. He runs it for a powerful consortium from back East."

"Ever hear of a gent named Keller?" Fargo asked, remembering the name Billy Pardee had mentioned.

Irish Mike absently nodded. "Who hasn't? Luther Keller is Prescott's right-hand man. Second in charge at the mine. Got his start as—" The door squeaked and Irish Mike paused. "Well, speak of the devil. Here he comes now."

Fargo turned. Into the saloon stalked a broad-shouldered man in a gray suit and bowler. He had a thick bull neck and fleshy jowls like those of a bulldog. A pencil-thin mustache framed his slit of a mouth, and on his chin grew a neatly trimmed triangle of a beard. In his shadow stepped a swarthy man in dark range clothes who favored an ivory-handled Smith & Wesson.

"Mr. Keller!" Irish Mike declared. "This is a pleasant surprise. You haven't graced me with a visit in, oh, a week or better."

"Then I'm overdue, aren't I?" Keller came over but the other man hung back near the entrance, his thumbs hooked in his gunbelt.

"Do you hear me complaining?" Irish Mike joked. "Will it be your usual? Bourbon?"

"That will be fine." Keller was studying Fargo intently without trying to be obvious, and was doing a poor job. "Hello," he said cordially. "I don't believe we've met."

"You're right," Fargo said, and poured himself another glass.

"Are you seeking work, by any chance?" Keller probed. "You don't strike me as a miner but we're always looking for good men at the Silverlode."

"No thanks." Fargo shifted. "But I did run into a gent from Texas earlier, camped east of here a ways. He wants to hire on with you. Said something about you needing men who are handy with guns." Curiosity more than anything else had prompted Fargo into fishing for information.

Luther Keller froze in the act of reaching for the bourbon. His jaw muscles twitching, he replied testily, "You must have been mistaken. What need would I have for short-trigger men? In case you haven't caught on yet, I'm in the mining business." He jerked a thumb at the dark man in the dark clothes. "Harvey there is the exception. We keep him on the payroll to deal with troublemakers."

"I heard that Texan plain as day," Fargo said. "He mentioned you by name. Strange that he didn't just ride on into town and ask around for you."

"And I say you're wrong." Keller tried hard not to show his agitation. He downed his drink in a couple of gulps, then slapped some coins onto the bar. "I'll thank you not to go spreading that tale of yours around Silver Flats. A man in my position can't afford to have baseless rumors spread."

Adjusting his bowler, he barreled on out with the swarthy gunman in tow.

"Now that was damned peculiar," Irish Mike remarked.

Fargo thought so, too, but he shrugged and carried the bottle to a table. "Any chance of getting a bite to eat?"

"I can have Flora make you something," Mike proposed. Cupping a hand to his mouth, he bellowed, "Flannigan! Get your adorable self out here! We've got us a paying customer!" He turned to Fargo, saying, "She's a feisty gal. Lost her husband in a cave-in last year and needed the work to help support her brood. Don't take liberties and she won't bash in your skull with a frying pan."

Both of them chuckled as a big-boned but winsome woman, whose mane of raven hair tumbled to her shapely buttocks came through the door. She wore a homespun dress that clung to her more than ample bosom and swaying hips. A scrubbed-clean complexion and lively hazel eyes completed the image. "A real, live paying customer you say? And here I reckoned we'd seen the last of them this century."

"Pay her no mind," Irish Mike said. "Her tongue is as tart as her food."

"Mike O'Shay, I'm the best cook in the territory, and you darn well know it," Flora scolded, wagging a finger at him in reproach. She stopped at Fargo's table. He caught the scent of lilacs clinging to her clothes. "So. By the process of elimination you must be the customer in question."

"And hungry enough to eat a buffalo," Fargo quipped.

"Well, unless you plan to go kill your own, you'll have to settle for eggs and bacon. And there's fresh baked pie for dessert. How would that be, big man?"

Fargo liked her playful gaze and frank bearing. "Throw in a pot of coffee and you have a deal. Add a back rub and I'll pay double."

Flora arched an eyebrow. "Would you indeed? If I thought that was a proposition, I'd pick up that chair next to you and hit you with it. I'm a lady. The last lecherous male who forgot that little fact lost four front teeth."

"Even ladies like company now and then," Fargo bantered.

"Ah. What a marvel. A man who claims he knows how women think." Flora's hazel eyes twinkled. "You're one in a million. Most men believe women were put on earth to bedevil and confuse them."

"And most women think men were put here to test their patience," Fargo countered. He was rewarded with a rich, lusty laugh.

"I like you, big man," the beauty confessed. "So I'll tell you what. For being such a sociable rascal, you can have that slice of pie at no extra charge."

Irish Mike overheard her. "Hold on there, Flora. This is my establishment and I set the prices, not you."

"True," Flora said, heading for the back, "but I do the cooking and the baking. So if I want to show a customer a wee bit of kindness, you'll not be stopping me, Mike O'Shay."

The door swung shut and Irish Mike shook his head in amazement. "Boyo, she must really be partial to you. She's never given another customer so much as a wink and a nod in all the time I've known her."

Fargo hoped it was an omen of things to come. Rising, he made for the entrance. "I'll stable my horse and be right back." He figured once the stallion was bedded down, he could relax and see about doing the same. Pushing the door wide, he stepped to the hitch rail and started to unwrap the pinto's reins. A glimmer of bright light on the roof of the building across the dusty street caught Fargo's attention and he looked up. Poking over the edge was a rifle barrel— pointed squarely at him.

Instinctively, Fargo dived to one side just as the rifle boomed. The slug bit into the dirt behind him, missing him and the Ovaro by inches. Palming his Colt, he snapped off two swift shots that splintered wood just below the rifle barrel and caused the rifleman to retreat from view. Heaving upright, Fargo rushed across the street.

A sign on the front of the building identified it as the assayer's office. Fargo was about to burst in through the door when he heard a loud thump at the rear. Veering to the left, Fargo flew around it to the back just in time to glimpse a vague figure vanish between buildings further down. He gave chase, sprinting past a ladder that had been propped against the wall.

As Fargo's legs raced, so did his mind. Who was trying to kill him? And why? He had no enemies in Silver Flats that he knew of. Luther Keller was angry at him over the comments he'd made in the saloon, yet they hardly merited being shot at.

Reaching the gap into which the would-be killer had vanished, Fargo dug in his heels. It was well he did. Again the rifle blasted, the bullet buzzing by like an angry hornet. Fargo banged off a shot of his own and heard boots pound in flight.

Again Fargo hurtled in pursuit. He caught sight of a leg rounding a corner, but when he reached the same spot, no one was in sight. He ran from building to building, checking alleys and every possible place of concealment, but after ten minutes he had to concede that the rifleman had given him the slip.

Twirling the Colt into its holster, Fargo returned to the main street. A small crowd, consisting mostly of women, had gathered near the saloon. Among them were Irish Mike and Flora, as well as Luther Keller. But not Harvey, Keller's hired gun.

A heavyset fellow in a beige hat, faded vest, baggy shirt, and loose-fitting pants, was telling everyone to stay calm, that there had to be a perfectly sound explanation for the shooting, and that he would get to the bottom of it. As Fargo approached, the man pivoted, revealing a battered badge pinned to his vest. "Hold it right there, mister. I'm

Fred Withers, town marshal. You wouldn't happen to know what all that ruckus was about, would you?"

Not breaking stride, Fargo looked straight at Luther Keller. "Someone tried to kill me."

Murmuring broke out, which the lawman hushed with a sharp gesture. "You don't say? Suppose we go to my office and you give me the details."

Fargo walked past Withers to the Ovaro. "Suppose you join me in the saloon and I'll tell you all about it over my meal." He checked to insure the slug hadn't nicked the pinto, then stroked its neck, deciding to leave it tied to the hitch rail for the time being.

Most of the onlookers were gazing at Withers, awaiting his response. "I reckon that's all right by me," he said.

Fargo had learned two important things about the lawman. One, Withers had less backbone than a snail. Why else had he stayed out in the street when he should have been investigating the gunfire? Any other town, the tin star would have come on the run, guns at the ready. Two, Withers was easily swayed. Most lawmen would tell Fargo his meal could wait and demand he go with them to the jail.

More whispering erupted as Fargo entered Irish Mike's and reclaimed his seat. Only this time, he turned the chair so he could see the entrance and the door to the kitchen. Whoever had tried to drygulch him might try again.

Fred Withers walked up, but before he could speak both Irish Mike and Flora were at Fargo's side talking at once.

"Who would want to make wolf meat of you, boyo?" the barkeep asked.

"Are you all right, big man? I can hold off on the food if it's spoiled your appetite," Flora offered.

Fargo took a swig of whiskey, then wiped his mouth with the back of his sleeve. "I don't know who shot at me. And I'm still hungry enough to eat a buffalo raw, so bring on those eggs, my dear."

As Flannigan and the proprietor moved off, the lawman pulled out a chair, saying, "I guess that answers my most important question. But I don't much like lead being slung in our streets. I run a quiet town, mister. On the weekend some of the miners can be a mite rowdy, but by and large Silver Flats is as peaceful as can be. There hasn't been a gunfight in a coon's age."

"It must make your job a lot easier," Fargo said.

Withers nodded. "And that's how I like it. Easy as can be. I don't much like gents who stir up trouble."

"Tell that to the bastard who tried to blow out my wick."

The lawman held up both hands, palm out. "I'm not accusing you of any wrongdoing. I'm just stating my policy. Which is why I'm afraid I'll have to ask you to leave town as soon as you're done eating."

Fargo thought about Keller and Harvey and Pardee. In his mind's eye, he then relived the moment when the rifleman fired at him from the roof. He recalled all too vividly how close he had come to being planted in an unmarked grave in the town cemetery. "No," he said.

Withers blinked. "No?"

"You heard me."

"But *you* must not have heard *me*. I'm not asking you, mister. I'm telling you. I want you out of Silver Flats. Whoever you are, you've brought trouble. Take it somewhere else. That's as plain as I can be."

"The answer is still no."

The lawman gnawed on his lower lip. At length he said, "I can deputize all the men I need to make you leave, whether you want to or not. There's still ten or eleven in town—more than enough to handle the likes of you."

"You won't, though."

"What makes you so sure?"

"You just said you don't like trouble. And if you try to throw me out, you'll have more trouble than a rat in a viper's nest." Fargo leaned on his elbows. "Since you laid your cards on the table, I'll do the same. I'm not going anywhere until I find out who tried to kill me and why."

"Listen," Withers said defensively, "you can't just ride

12

on in here and act like you're the cock of the roost. We abide by the letter of the law."

Fargo was tired of his carping. "Is it against the law for me to stay as long as I want?" he demanded.

"Technically, no, but—"

"Then you're wasting your breath. Go pester someone else. Or, better yet, track down the man who shot at me and I'll be out of your hair that much sooner." Fargo extended the bottle. "Care for a drink before you go?"

Peeved, Withers shoved his chair back and stood. "I don't think I like you very much, mister. You can stick around for now, though. If there's any more gunplay, however, you'll regret being so pushy. I'll only bend so far."

"That's good to hear," Fargo said, and meant it.

No sooner had the lawman tromped off than Flora swayed out, bearing a coffeepot and a cup and saucer on a tray. "The eggs will be ready in a minute." She set the tray down, regarding him with lively interest. "Tell me, big man. Do you have a place to stay tonight?"

"Not yet. Why?"

Flora bent so her luscious mouth was inches from his. "I happen to have a spare room which you're more than welcome to use. Interested?"

"Very much so," Fargo replied, marveling at the turn of events. He remembered thinking that Silver Flats must be dull. How wrong he'd been. In less than an hour someone had tried to murder him and a lovely woman was inviting him to spend the night.

What next?

2

The sun had set over an hour ago. Silver Flat's streets were quieter than ever, with hardly anyone out and about. In three days that would change, when the miners thronged down from the Silverlode for the weekend.

Skye Fargo was looking for the address Flora Flannigan had given him when a furtive movement and the crunch of leaves alerted him that he was being followed. He slowed, shifting the Henry from his right hand to his left so he could draw the Colt. Over his left shoulder were his saddlebags. His saddle and bedroll were at the stable, being looked after by the stableman.

Fargo spied the two-story yellow frame house belonging to Flora up ahead. It was the last one on the side street, bordered by a neat picket fence and a flower garden. Beyond lay foothills and the high mountains in all their regal majesty, their snowy crowns glistening in the light of the half-moon.

Another rustling noise brought Fargo around in a whirl. He flashed the Colt up and out, his thumb curling back the hammer even as his finger closed on the trigger. But he didn't shoot. Instead, he glowered at a sprout of nine or ten years old who had frozen in abject fright a hand's-width from the revolver's muzzle. "What the hell is the matter with you, boy? Sneaking up on a person like that could get you killed."

"Golly, mister. Timmy didn't mean no harm."

Fargo swiveled to find a girl of twelve or so. Beside her

was another girl not much over six, gaping in wide-eyed amazement.

"Molly's right," chimed in someone else. "We were just eager to see you, is all. Ma hasn't had a man over since Pa passed on."

Two more youngsters, both boys, one slightly older than Molly and one a couple of years younger, had risen from the bushes. "Are you Flora's kids?" Fargo asked.

"Yes, sir," the tallest boy said. "I'm Sam, this here is Orville, over there by Molly is little Susie. Timmy is the one whose head you almost blew off."

"All five of you?"

"What's wrong with that?" Sam rejoined. "Mr. and Mrs. Webster have seven kids. The Deavers have nine. Compared to them, five ain't much of a litter."

Molly, who wore her hair in braids and had a dimple in the middle of her chin, stepped forward and offered Fargo a rose, no doubt plucked from their mother's flower bed. "Ma said we were to greet you proper, so we picked this." She nodded at the pistol. "You're not still fixing to shoot us, are you?"

Feeling immensely foolish, Fargo replaced the Colt and accepted the gift. "Thank you, kind lady."

Giggling, Molly motioned to her siblings. "Don't be scared. He isn't so bad. Jumpy as a bobcat on hot rocks, maybe, but who wouldn't be with someone trying to make worm food of you."

"You know about that?"

Sam snorted. "Heck, mister. The whole town has heard. It's all anyone has been talking about. Some say you're a badman on the run. Some say you ought to be tarred and feathered." He paused. "But Ma says you're a nice fella and we should be on our best behavior or she'll tan our backsides."

Fargo sniffed the rose. "What do you five think?"

"You look like an Injun fighter to me," Sam said.

"I think you're cute," Molly declared.

Orville couldn't take his eyes off the Colt. "I bet you're a gunman. Will you teach me how to draw like you just did so I can shoot a lot of people when I grow up?"

Little Susie, too shy to speak, peeked out at him from behind Molly.

That left Timmy, who announced to one and all, "I was so scared, I wet my pants. Ma will throw a fit."

"I'll explain to her," Fargo said, although what help that would be was anyone's guess. Most mothers didn't appreciate having revolvers shoved into the faces of their pride and joys.

Molly surprised Fargo by taking his hand and leading him toward the gate. "We sure are excited to have you visit. Ma made us clean the house from end to end. We even had to sweep under our beds and hang up all our clothes."

"She hasn't gone to this much bother since the parson and his wife came for dinner," Sam revealed.

"Will you shoot something for us?" Orville requested. "A fence post will do. Or how about one of our windows?"

"I smell like the hind end of a horse," Timmy threw in.

Molly held the gate open. Ringed by the children, Fargo walked up the narrow gravel path to the front porch. By the light spilling through a window he saw they had been scrubbed spotless. Their hair had been washed and neatly combed. All were wearing their best Sunday clothes, too. "I thank you for your hospitality."

Orville scratched his head. "Shucks, this ain't no hospital, mister. It's our home."

"He meant our kindness, you yack," Molly said. "Don't you know anything?" She scooted to the door and worked the latch. "After you. Ma says you're to make yourself at home. She's in the kitchen cooking."

"She's been slaving over that hot stove since she got home," Sam reported. "Got herself all made up in her prettiest dress, too. She even took a bath in broad daylight."

"Samuel!" Molly scolded. "Show some manners. Ladies

don't like to talk about that sort of thing in mixed company."

"What sort of thing?" Sam asked, genuinely perplexed.

"Baths, stupid."

"What's wrong with that? Everyone takes them. Except Old Man Walker, that is. He says baths are bad for you, and they give you colds and such. He likes to brag that he hasn't had one since he was in diapers. Maybe that's why he smells so bad."

"He's not the only one," Timmy said.

Samuel looked at Fargo. "How often do you take a bath, mister?"

"How about shooting a few holes in the wall?" Orville pleaded. "Ma won't mind if they're small ones."

Fargo was spared having to answer either question by the timely arrival of Flora Flannigan. She swished into the sitting room in a store-bought dress that accented her bosom and rustled with every motion of her finely outlined thighs. Her raven tresses shone, her lips cherry red. A vanilla scent wafted from her like sweet fragrance did from the rose. She was lovely enough to set any man's mouth to watering.

"Nice to see you again," Fargo said.

Flora had her hands on her hips, and gave her offspring a motherly appraisal. "I heard all that chatter. There will be no badgering our guest, do you hear me? Molly, you go set the table. Susie, you help. Orville, I don't want to hear any more about putting holes in our walls. Sam, bring in some wood for the stove. And Timmy"—Flora sniffed—"why in the world did you wet your britches?"

"That was my fault," Fargo said, and detailed the incident. "I'm sorry."

"No need to apologize," Flora said. "I'd be skittish, too, under the circumstances. But do us all a favor. If our cat jumps on your lap without warning, don't shoot her."

"Aww, Ma," Orville said. "We can always get another."

"Go help Timmy change his pants," Flora directed.

Suddenly, the two grownups were alone. "You have quite

a handful," Fargo commented, thinking that she would be quite a handful herself.

Flora's smile radiated affection. "That I do. And I'm right proud of every one of the rascals. They're the only things my dear husband left me free and clear, God rest his poor soul."

"I hear he died in a mine accident. For what it's worth, I'm sorry."

"An accident my—" Flora started, and caught herself. "This isn't the right time to be discussing Flynn's death. It would only spoil my mood. So come, Mr. Fargo. The food is done. If you don't mind, we'll eat right away. We'll have time to ourselves later." She clasped his hand. "I promise."

All the rooms, Fargo saw, contained the barest of furnishings. The family's income had never been all that great to begin with, and the loss of Flora's husband had strapped the family severely. Even so, Flora had done her best to make the table as elegant as she could, with a new tablecloth and folded napkins and silverware shined to a sparkle. She seated Fargo at the head of the table, and as he sank down some of the children shot him troubled looks. He knew what they were thinking. It was the chair their father always used, one they never sat in themselves. For someone else to use it didn't seem right. "Would you rather I sat somewhere else?" he asked Molly, who appeared most stricken.

"Oh, no, sir," the oldest girl replied. "That's fine. I was just remembering Pa, is all."

The meal was fit for royalty. Chicken soup and hot rolls, then a salad and the main course of beef, potatoes, and carrots. Fargo realized Flora had spent a lot of money on his behalf. Dessert was a cake, as delicious as any ever baked.

The children were in fine spirits and chattered like squirrels. They besieged Fargo with questions about the places he had traveled and if he had lived among Indians. Had he ever been to St. Louis? To California? Did the ocean really taste salty? Was it true Comanches were part horse and part human? Did Apaches really eat people alive?

"That will be quite enough," Flora finally said. "We didn't invite him over to pester him silly."

"Just a couple more, Ma. Please?" Molly begged. "There's something I've got to know."

"I don't mind," Fargo said.

Flora nodded, and Molly squealed in delight. "What are the ladies wearing nowadays in places like Denver and the other big cities? Mr. Simms down at the general store doesn't have much of a selection. All we have to go by is a musty old catalog."

Fargo described some of the latest fashions. The boys fidgeted and showed about as much interest as they would in a knitting class. But Molly and Flora and even little Susie hung on every word. They plied him with queries, and he answered each one to the best of his ability. When he mentioned the latest fad—the crinoline—an impish gleam came into Flora's eyes.

"Mercy me, but you sure do know an awful lot about women's garments. It makes a body wonder how it is you came by your vast store of knowledge."

All the children looked at him. Damned if Fargo didn't start to feel himself blush, and to hide it, he lifted his water glass and drank it dry.

Flora laughed. "I'm sorry. I didn't mean to embarrass you. It's unfair of us to ask a man to talk about such things. Most don't care what their women wear. A wife could go around in a burlap bag with holes cut in it and the husband would be perfectly happy so long as the food was on the table when he wanted it and his feet were warm at night."

"His feet, Ma?" Molly asked.

"That's right, dear. Men think they have the God-given right to shove their cold feet between their wives's legs any time they want. Even your wonderful father was marred by that particular flaw." Flora quivered at the memory. "I'd wake up covered with goosebumps and couldn't get back to sleep for ages."

"Men sure can be rude," Molly said in disbelief.

"Ah, child. The list of their atrocious habits is longer than my arm and leg combined. Why we inflict them on ourselves is beyond me." Flora winked at Fargo.

"My husband won't be like that," Molly stated with conviction. "I'll train him not to do things I don't like. And to help with the dishes. And to clean up after himself."

Throaty mirth pealed from Flora. "My sweet angel, women have been trying to train men since the Garden of Eden. Show me one who says she's succeeded and I'll show you the biggest liar this side of the Emerald Isle. Men are incapable of being taught new tricks. They'd rather lounge about and be waited on hand and foot."

Molly glanced at Fargo. "Is that true?"

"This sure is delicious cake," Fargo said, trying to wriggle off the hook.

Flora laughed louder. Little Susie joined in although she had no idea what she was laughing at. The boys looked bored, and Orville took advantage of the lull in conversation to bring up something that must have been on the tip of his tongue all night.

"Have you ever killed anyone, Mr. Fargo?"

"Orville Flannigan!" Flora scolded. "What has gotten into you? It's improper to pry into someone's personal life, and especially about matters that don't concern you."

"I'm sorry, Ma," Orville said, then promptly asked Fargo, "Have you? My pa never did. He wouldn't even carry a gun unless it was a rifle to hunt with. He used to say that killing was bad. But people do it all the time. Marshal Withers shot a man once, an outlaw, a long time ago—"

Flora was indignant. "That will be quite enough out of you, young man! I'm quite certain our guest doesn't care to discuss it."

Fargo speared another piece of cake with his fork but he didn't lift it to his mouth. All the children were staring at him expectantly. He felt obligated to say something. "Your father was a wise man. It would be nice if everyone believed like he did. No one would ever be shot or stabbed. But there are a lot of people who like to hurt others. I hope you never run into anyone like that and have to do as Marshal Withers did." They resumed eating, with no one seeming to notice that he had avoided the issue entirely.

Except Flora, who smiled warmly.

After supper they repaired to the living room and the children enticed Fargo into a game of cards called old maid. Molly was a wizard at it and won most of the time. In a rocking chair in the corner Flora watched in amusement, humming to herself.

Fargo hoped she wasn't getting any wrong notions. He was as fond of kids as the next person but he had no desire to have any of his own. Not when there were so many sights yet to see, so many places yet to visit. As he laid down a ten of hearts, he remarked, "You're a fine cook. Why do you stick it out here in Silver Flats when you could easily get a better-paying job in any big city?"

"It's not by choice," Flora said rather sadly. "To move takes money. I scrimp and save as best as I can, but with so many mouths to feed it'll be another year or two before I have enough to cover our expenses and ship all our belongings."

"Why not sell them and buy new ones later?"

"My husband and I worked hard to get what little we had, Skye. This rocking chair? He worked overtime for two months just to be able to give it to me for a present. Most everything else has a memory attached to it as well." Flora sighed. "I just can't bring myself to part with any of it. I'm being silly, I know. But that's how I feel, and I've always been one to live by my feelings."

Samuel, taking forever to decide which card to play, chimed in, "Ma says we need a thousand dollars. Once she saves that much we're going to St. Louis."

"On a riverboat!" Molly said excitedly. "In our own cabins and everything!"

They were too young to perceive the truth. Fargo knew their mother would never be able to save that much, not in Silver Flats, with six mouths to feed and a roof to keep over their heads. St. Louis was a dream, the glue that bonded their mutual hope of a better life, of better times. A dream that might turn bitter once the children matured and realized it for what it was. Fargo would hate to see that happen.

After old maid came checkers. Fargo beat Sam and Molly and was letting Susie beat him when Flora rose and announced it was bedtime. The children groused, stalling as long as possible before reluctantly tramping off to bed.

Molly surprised Fargo by impulsively giving him a peck on the cheek. "We sure do like you."

"They're not the only ones," Flora said when they were finally alone. She had switched from the rocking chair to the divan, her legs dangling almost at his elbow. "You've made an impression none of us will soon forget. Not since Flynn—" Stopping, she bowed her head.

"What were you going to tell me about his accident?" Fargo asked.

"Oh. Just that it wasn't. An accident, I mean. Flynn was too smart, too careful, to do as Luther Keller claimed." Flora's features hardened. "Keller! Now there's a polecat if ever there was one. My husband hadn't been in the ground two weeks and Keller started hinting that he and I should go on late night buggy rides."

"How exactly did Flynn die?" Fargo pressed her, quickly adding, "If you'd rather not talk about it, I'll understand."

"No, no. It's all right. I have to learn to deal with the loss sooner or later, don't I?" Flora took a deep breath. "Flynn had been at the Silverlode longer than just about anyone except Mr. Prescott, who runs it, and Luther Keller, who just acts as if he does. Prescott is the kindest soul you'd ever want to meet and he thought highly of my Flynn. But Flynn and Keller never hit it off."

"Was it because of Keller's interest in you?"

Flora shook her head. "Keller never showed any interest before Flynn died. No, my husband didn't like how Keller bossed the men around as if they were slaves. And when Mr. Prescott put Flynn in charge of one of the work crews, it got worse. Keller and Flynn were always arguing over how best to get the work done."

"And you think Keller had him killed?"

"Not over their disagreements, no. But three days before Flynn died, he came home one weekend and wouldn't say much. I could tell he was upset but he wouldn't confide why. Which was unusual. Ordinarily he shared everything with me. All he would say was that it was better if I didn't know."

"He didn't give you any clue at all?"

"Just that he was going to have a talk with Mr. Prescott on Monday and there would be some big changes at the mine." Flora's eyes began to mist over. "He never had that talk, though. He went to work on Monday morning, and Tuesday morning a wagon came rattling up to our front gate. It was Wayne Arnold, a good friend of Flynn's. There had been a cave-in, and Mr. Prescott sent Wayne to fetch me." Her voice broke.

Fargo placed a comforting hand on her knee, the warmth of her leg tingling his palm. "Maybe you should finish the story later."

"I'm a big girl. I can handle it." Flora covered his hand with hers. "Mrs. Deaver offered to watch the kids and Charlie rushed me up to the mine, but as soon as we arrived I knew we were too late. There was a body wrapped in canvas by the entrance. It was Flynn. They'd dug him out about half an hour before I got there."

"How long does it take to reach the Silverlode from town?"

"What? Oh, about six hours. The mine is only twenty miles away but it's a steep climb the last ten, with a lot of switchbacks. That's why the men stay up there all week and only come down for the weekends. It's too long a trip to make twice a day."

"Go on," Fargo coaxed.

"There's not much left to tell. According to Luther Keller, Flynn had gone into a shaft they were digging. It hadn't been properly shored up yet, and it came crashing down on top of him."

"Cave-ins do happen."

"You think I don't know that? Losing her man to those damnable mines is every wife's worst nightmare! But Flynn would never go into a shaft that wasn't safe. He insisted on safety above all else." Flora's grip on Fargo's hand tightened until it was almost painful. "Keller claimed Flynn was inspecting the shaft to see what shoring needed to be done. But that wasn't Flynn's job. It was someone else's."

"What did George Prescott say?"

"He accepted Keller's word. Why shouldn't he? He never knew about the trouble between them. Mr. Prescott called it a tragic accident and did his best to comfort me. He even went so far as to give us two months' worth of Flynn's pay. Of course, most of it went toward the funeral. I wanted it done right, with a decent coffin and all."

The more Fargo learned, the more his conviction grew that Luther Keller was up to no good. But the exact nature of Keller's scheme eluded him. His encounter with Pardee, the attempt on his life, and now the details of Flynn's death all hinted that whatever Keller was after, the men believed it valuable enough to kill for.

"I've been so alone," Flora unexpectedly said. Raising both hands to her temples, she massaged them. "Sometimes I get so tense, so worried."

In the golden glow of the lamp her raven hair shone like black gold, her full figure like ripe fruit waiting to be plucked. Fargo moved his hand higher on her leg and she didn't protest. In fact, she parted her thighs slightly. "It's rough raising five kids alone," he said.

"You don't know the half of it, handsome. There's not

many jobs for women. Decent jobs, anyway. I was lucky Irish Mike let me go to work for him." Flora gazed at the stairs leading to the second floor. "But you know what? I wouldn't trade a minute of motherhood for all the tea in China. They're my darling angels, every one of the little rascals. I'd die before I'd give them up."

"It will take a miracle to save up the thousand dollars you want," Fargo commented.

"Not one to mince words, are you, big man?" Flora said. "I know that, and you know that, but do me a favor and never, ever tell my children. They have their hearts set on a new life in St. Louis." She paused. "We all need our dreams, but children more so than the rest of us."

Fargo squeezed her leg. "You're a remarkable woman, Flora Flannigan."

"And a lonely one," Flora reiterated. Bending down, she kissed him full on the mouth, her lips warm and soft and tasting faintly like strawberries.

"Why me?" Fargo quizzed when she broke for air.

Flora traced the outline of his jaw with a fingernail. "Didn't anyone ever tell you not to look a gift horse in the mouth?" She pecked him on the forehead. "Maybe it's because you're the handsomest cuss to come along in ages. Maybe it's because you treated me kindly, and didn't try to paw me like so many do at the saloon. Maybe it's because my children have taken a shine to you." She rimmed her cherry lips with the tip of her tongue. "And maybe it's because I've been hungry for companionship for many months now, and you stir feelings I haven't felt since Flynn was alive."

Fargo rose onto the divan beside her, sitting so their legs brushed together. "I'll take that as a compliment." He began to lean toward her to take her into his arms, then sensed another presence in the room.

Little Susie was at the bottom of the stairs, rubbing her eyes. "Ma, I need a drink. My throat is dry."

"I almost forgot," Flora said softly to Fargo. "She always

comes back down shortly after turning in. Sort of a ritual. Give me a minute."

It took five. Flora apologized profusely as she sat back down, informing him, "I checked. All the others are sound asleep. We won't be disturbed again."

Fargo hoped not, because the kiss and her perfume and her voluptuous body were stirring a hunger of his own. He pulled her toward him, locking his mouth to hers, their tongues entwining in a silken swirl of unchecked need that ended abruptly when she pushed back, flushed and breathing heavily.

"Mercy! I feel so hot, I'm burning up."

"Let me feel for myself," Fargo said, and without further delay took both of her breasts in his hands.

3

When Flora Flannigan described herself as hungry for male companionship, she had not been exaggerating. She molded herself to Skye Fargo with fiery passion, her hands roaming the length of his body, her mouth an inferno, searing him with exquisite pleasure. He felt her breasts straining against the fabric of her dress as if seeking to rip through the material. Her thighs ground against his, her mound radiating heat like a miniature sun. She craved him with every fiber in her being, and it showed.

Fargo was flattered. Their coupling was terrifically intense, supremely exciting, and marvelously stimulating. He pinched one of her nipples and she just about shot off the divan. Their tongues were tied together. She panted as he gently eased her down onto her back, then stripped off his gunbelt and laid it on the floor.

Flora gave him a strange look.

"Something wrong?" Fargo asked.

Her gaze strayed on high. "I just hope my sweet Flynn can forgive me. I'm only human. And it's been so long, so awfully long."

"Would you rather we didn't?"

Flora's answer was to slide a hand behind his neck and yank him down on top of her. Her mouth melded with his as Fargo slid his hands to her breasts. His knee sank between her spreading legs and pressed against her searing core. She reacted by clamping her thighs around him.

"Ohhhh, Skye," Flora cooed when Fargo lowered his

mouth to lick her left earlobe. She wriggled deliciously, her hands running through his hair and over his broad back. "You have no idea how this makes me feel."

She was wrong. Fargo began to undo the buttons at the top of her dress, parting it so he could gain access to her womanly charms underneath. Soon he was pulling her clothes aside, exposing her melon-shaped breasts in all their superb, smooth-as-glass glory. They were round and full and oh-so-inviting. He swooped to the left one, then the right, dallying at each, lavishing them with equal attention.

Flora loved it. She squirmed and bucked, mashing herself against him in carnal abandon. Her raven hair had spilled over her shoulders, framing her lovely face. Wantonly, her hands roamed to his backside and she fondled him.

A tingle shot up Fargo's spine. He hiked up the lower half of her dress, raising it as high as her knees. Her legs were nicely shaped, Fargo noted, firm and supple. He stroked her calves awhile, then caressed higher, rubbing her thighs but not venturing higher. He wanted to prolong the suspense in order to heighten her enjoyment.

"Please," Flora mewed in due coarse. "Oh, please!"

Fargo slid his hand to the junction of her thighs. His knuckles brushed her wet slit, and she threw her head back, her mouth opened wide, and groaned long and loud. Too loud, evidently, for she quickly pressed her face into the divan to smoother her cries.

She didn't want to awaken her children, and Fargo made a mental note to follow her example. He rubbed his forefinger up and down and around, but he didn't enter her yet, teasing her with the prospect of what was to come. Not until he was good and ready would he commit himself. He wanted her quivering with uncontrollable lust. So he stoked her as if she were a furnace, making her inner heat rise, her temperature climbing feverishly. Her body sizzled with raw need when at last he thrust his finger inside her.

"Ahhhhh!" Flora exclaimed, and again she pressed her

face to the divan while her hips pumped violently against his hand.

It was all Fargo could do to hold on to her. He fed in another finger, and just like that she exploded, her inner walls rippling and contracting. She lunged upward, seeking his mouth, and Fargo kissed her.

Flora's nipples were now as hard as nails. Her inner thighs were drenched. She had her knees crooked and was pumping against him in a regular rhythm, matching the strokes of his arm. "More," she husked. "Please, more."

Fargo had no intention of stopping any time soon. He swirled his fingers, provoking her to surge off the divan so high, she nearly threw both of them to the floor. Her fingernails bit into his shoulders and raked at his back. Her burning lips devoured his cheek, his neck, his throat.

To Fargo's mild surprise, Flora suddenly shoved a hand into his pants, slipping her fingers around his throbbing member. Her fingers played across his pole, lightly, delicately. She worked her hand a few times, causing his throat to constrict and his manhood to strain. He had to grit his teeth to keep from losing control prematurely. It was his turn to groan, and he bit his lower lip to stifle it.

"So big," Flora said softly. "So long." Greedily, she undid his buckskin pants and eagerly pushed them down around his knees. "So beautiful."

Fargo lowered his mouth to hers. The feel of her hand on him was sheer bliss. His hands explored every nook and cranny, every smooth expanse of her. She was any man's innermost dream come true, a treasure trove of sensual delight.

Flora didn't just lie there like a bump on a log. Her fingers knowingly brought Fargo to the summit just as he had done with her. They coasted in ethereal bliss, adrift in a sea of ecstasy.

Fargo had reached the point where he couldn't stop if his life depended on it. If any of the children came downstairs, they'd learn about the favorite pastime of adults sooner than Flora had counted on. He rubbed the tip of his pole up and down her opening and she uttered a throaty purr.

"Do it now or I'll go crazy."

Aligning himself, Fargo tensed, then drove up into her. Flora gripped his upper arms, her legs wrapping around his waist. She wasn't letting him go come hell or high water. For several seconds they lay perfectly still, savoring the moment. The spell was broken when Fargo rocked on his knees, the friction of his shaft against her wet inner walls creating an erotic rhythm all their own.

Fargo lost all track of the passage of time. Afloat in a sea of enhanced sensation, he didn't want it to ever end. Apparently Flora felt likewise. She clung to him as a drowning person would cling to a log, like someone whose very being depended on the contact of their two plunging forms. They were both breathing heavily like two thoroughbreds in a race, only in this case they were surging toward mutual release, toward the pinnacle of sexual rapture.

Flora crested first. Her muscles constricting and her repeated breathless sighs preceding her release. Her ankles hooked behind his back for added leverage as she surged against him. Eyelids fluttering, Flora threw back her head and opened her mouth in a silent shriek.

Fargo's own climax wasn't long in coming. It built up at the base of his spine, swelling like a tidal wave until containing it was no longer possible. Then the room tilted and whirled and dazzling pinpoints of light flared before his eyes. Pure rapture overcame him from head to toe.

Gradually they coasted to a stop. Fargo was spent, Flora was as limp as a doll, one arm and a leg hanging over the divan. He collapsed on top of her, his cheek cushioned by her soft mounds. Were it up to him, he'd have lain there for hours, at peace with the world. But after a few minutes she nudged him and whispered in his ear.

"I'm so sorry. But the children—"

"Say no more," Fargo whispered. Rolling onto the floor,

he hitched up his pants, then sprawled onto his stomach, too relaxed to do much else.

"You were magnificent," Flora said.

"So were you," Fargo complimented her. He was telling the truth. She truly was extraordinary. Women who weren't ashamed of their sexual nature were all too rare, as he well knew.

"I suppose I should show you to your room," Flora said, composing herself.

Fargo hadn't expected her to let him have his way with her on the divan when it would be much safer in a bedroom. But once upstairs, he learned why she hadn't objected. The spare room was right next to the room in which Samuel, Orville, and Timmy slept. Across from it was the bedroom shared by her daughters.

"I hope this will do," Flora said.

It was as Spartan as the rest of the house but the bed was more comfortable than any Fargo would find in a hotel. Depositing his belongings in a corner, he hugged Flora and they shared a lingering kiss.

"Oh, you make me warm and tingly inside. For two bits I'd throw you down and have you ravish me again."

"What's stopping you?" Fargo teased.

"Not up here," Flora said. "Those little devils of mine can hear a pin drop. Except when I'm calling them in to supper or need them to do chores. Then they turn as deaf as stone." She caressed his chin, smiled, and left him, closing the door behind her.

Fargo threw his hat onto a dresser, removed his spurs and boots and stretched out on the bed. He should undress, he told himself, but he was feeling too spent, too content. A good meal, a good woman, and a good home. He could see why some men were so eager to get hitched and rear families. There was a lot to be said for married life. Not that he had any inclination to let a woman snare him any time soon.

Dozing off, Fargo dreamed of being married to Flora. In

his dream, they had twelve kids instead of five, and the children were always running around like a pack of frenzied banshees, screaming and fighting and making a mess. He kept hollering at them to behave but everything he said went in one ear and out the other. Then he heard a squeal and ran out back to find two of the boys poking the Ovaro with sticks. Incensed, he picked them up and was about to dump them in the water trough when he woke up.

Fargo chuckled. So much for married life! He sat up to remove his shirt, then paused. From downstairs came a scuffling noise; then a sound he couldn't identify. He wondered if the squeal he had heard in his dream had been a real sound and not just his imagination. Deciding his imagination was getting the better of him, he started to put on his shirt.

The sound came again. Snatching the Colt, Fargo opened his door to listen. He heard nothing other than one of the children snoring lightly, yet he couldn't shake the persistent feeling that something was amiss. Moving silently to the head of the stairs, he hesitated. The lights were still on. Flora was probably tidying up before turning in. What would she think if he rushed down there with his gun out?

Then Fargo heard a chair scrape, followed by a distinct slap. He took the stairs two at a time, making no noise in his socks. At the bottom he crouched and slid along the wall to the kitchen. The door was partway open and through it he could see Flora in one of the chairs, held down by a man who wore a bandanna over the lower half of his face. Two other gunmen were beside her, also wearing bandannas. One was bent down, jabbing a finger into her.

"—lie to us again, bitch! Where is he?"

Flora had a red handprint on her cheek. Her hair was disheveled and her arms were being bent at a painful angle by the first man. But she jutted her chin in defiance, saying, "I'll tell you again, you miserable weasel, that you're mistaken. The only ones here are my children and myself."

"We know you're lying," the gunman said. "We've been spying on him. We saw him come in with his stuff, and he never left. So unless you want those precious brats of yours hurt, you'll tell us which room he's in."

"Don't you dare lay a finger on my children!" Flora declared, trying to rise, but she was roughly slammed down again.

The gunman straightened. He was a broomstick with dark eyes and unwashed hair that jutted out from under a dirty brown hat. "Whether we do or not is up to you, lady. We're only being paid to kill him. But if you don't stop giving us guff—" he shrugged. "Don't blame us for what happens."

Flora had tears in her eyes. Whether from fury or dismay Fargo couldn't say. Straightening, he slowly eased the door wide. The gunmen had no inkling of his presence until he cocked the Colt.

"Not one twitch or you're dead."

Two of the men froze but the scruffy scarecrow glanced over his shoulder. "Well, ain't this cozy? In your stockinged feet, no less. Did the widow-lady make you feel right to home?" He snickered at his joke.

"Shuck those gunbelts," Fargo intsructed them.

"We can't do that and you know it," the scruffy gunman replied. "The smart thing for you to do is let us back on out. Otherwise, this pretty lady might take a stray slug."

The man had a point. Even if Fargo put a bullet into each of them before they cleared leather, they still might get off a shot or two. Flora might be hit. Or a slug might rip through the ceiling and into the bedrooms above, striking one of the children.

"What will it be, mister?" the scarecrow asked. "You have my range word we won't shoot if you don't."

Fargo trusted him about as far as he could fling a bull elk. But what other choice was there? "Keep your hands where I can see them. No sudden moves. And once you're out that door, all bets are off."

Smirking, the scruffy gunman started backing away. "I wouldn't have it any other way, big man. Landing you in a shallow grave will please my boss greatly. Show him that I can be relied on."

The cutthroat holding Flora let go and backpedaled. The third one was slow to leave, his expression telling Fargo he would rather resort to his hardware than turn tail.

It didn't go unnoticed. "Don't be a jackass, Mull," the scruffy gunman said. "He's got us dead to rights. Wait until we're outside."

"I don't back down for anyone," Mull said gruffly.

"The boss put me in charge. So do as I say, damn it!" The scarecrow was almost to the back door.

Fargo sidled to the right for a clearer shot, risking a glance at Flora. She caught his eye and bobbed her chin at the floor. Before he could shake his head, she flung herself from the chair.

"Now, Skye! Now!"

All three gunmen stabbed for their six-guns. Fargo triggered a shot into Mull, who was closest to Flora, then pivoted as he fanned the hammer of the Colt. Hot lead smashed into the second gunman's stomach, doubling him over.

That left their scruffy leader, who had drawn his pistol with one hand while working the latch with the other. They both fired at the same instant. The gunman's slug ripped into the wall beside Fargo. Whether Fargo scored or not was uncertain, for in the next second the gunman had pushed the door open and dashed into the darkness.

Fargo would have gone after him but the other two were still alive, and still game. Mull had produced a revolver so Fargo cored his chest, knocking him against a chair. But it wasn't enough. Mull tottered, his brawny arms sagging, yet he still fired blindly, one shot after another, most down low toward the floor—and Flora.

The table screened her from Fargo's view. Forgetting himself, he started to rush around it while sending another slug into Mull. The stubborn killer oozed to the floor. But the other gunman had recovered enough to point a pistol. In pure reflex, Fargo shot him through the head.

"Flora?" Fargo stepped past the table. She was face-down, not moving, her raven locks spilled across her dress.

"Is it safe?" she asked, rolling over.

Splintered holes in the floor showed how close she had come to meeting her Maker. "Stay down," Fargo cautioned, and ran to the doorway. Almost too late he remembered the Colt was empty and that he hadn't brought his gunbelt. He couldn't reload. Darting to the gunman by the wall, he snatched up the man's pistol. It hadn't been fired, and there were five pills in the wheel. More than enough.

Wedging the empty Colt under his belt, Fargo raced out the back door, hunched low. Flame stabbed the night. A bullet smacked the wall. Fargo snapped off a slug of his own, aiming at the flash in the dark, and then immediately slanted to the right. Again the scruffy scarecrow fired. Like Fargo, he had changed position. Fargo banged off another shot, took several more steps, and squatted.

No telltale movement gave the man's location away. Back in the house, some of the children were shrieking in a panic, drowning out any sounds the gunman might make. Thwarted, Fargo ventured further.

Shouts came from nearby homes. Windows filled with light. It wouldn't be long before the neighbors investigated.

Fargo looked toward the street. At the limit of his vision, a sprinting figure was there, and then it was gone. He stood to give chase but thought better of the idea. The scruffy gunman had too much of a head start.

Returning to the house, Fargo halted on the threshold. All the children were there in their pajamas, Molly gawking, little Susie being comforted by her mother, Timmy clutching tightly to a small toy stuffed rabbit, and Samuel acting unsure whether he should be excited or scared. Orville, grinning, was mesmerized by the splattered blood and brains.

"You shouldn't be looking at that," Fargo said, going in.

Orville didn't stop. "You shot these fellas and I wasn't here to see it! Why couldn't you do it when I was around?"

Flora picked up Susie. "That will be quite enough out of you, young man. I want all of you back in your beds this instant."

"Aw, Ma," Orville said. "How often do we get to see dead badmen?"

"Run along!" Flora commanded. "Any minute now some of our neighbors are bound to show up. You're to stay upstairs, you hear me?"

Orville grumbled but dutifully trailed his siblings out of the kitchen. Flora handed Susie to Molly as shouts arose from the front of the house, coming closer.

"I'm sorry," Fargo said. "I didn't mean to bring this down on your head."

"How were you to know?" Flora responded. Biting her lower lip, she fluffed at her hair, trying to make herself more presentable. "Don't blame yourself."

But Fargo did. He should have realized that whoever had sicced the rifleman on him would try again. He'd have been better off, and Flora's family a lot safer, if he had bedded down in the stable. Tossing the gunman's pistol onto the table, he hurried upstairs to put on his boots, gunbelt, and hat. When he came back down, the living room was filled, mostly with women bundled in long robes and a few men in nightshirts. All of them were besieging Flora with questions but they fell silent when Fargo appeared.

An older, prudish woman with a hooked nose regarded him with ill-concealed contempt. "Is this the one? Why was he upstairs? Don't tell me he's *staying* with you?" She made it sound like the original sin.

"I'm letting him use the spare bedroom for the night," Flora explained.

"A man alone with you in your home?" the woman said. "What were you thinking? It's scandalous."

Flora clenched her fists. "I'll thank you to keep your wicked thoughts to yourself, Miss Henderson."

A portly man in a striped nightshirt held up a pudgy hand. "Ladies, ladies! That's hardly the issue. There's been a gunfight. Men are dead in your kitchen, Mrs. Flannigan. I saw them with my own eyes."

"I sent my son for the marshal," someone else mentioned.

Then everyone was jabbering at the same time, some demanding to know why Flora had let Fargo stay, others wanting to know why the shooting had taken place, or commenting on how unseemly the whole affair was. Fargo planted himself at the bottom of the stairs and bellowed, "Who do I shoot next?"

Another hush descended.

"What did you just say?" the portly man asked.

"Mrs. Flannigan has been through enough," Fargo said. "She needs peace and quiet, as do the children. So all of you will clear out. Now."

The prude pulled her robe tighter and huffed, "Well, I never!"

"No wonder you're a spinster," Fargo said. "Now get out! Every last one of you."

Casting spiteful looks and muttering among themselves, the neighbors tromped onto the porch and into the yard. Fargo moved to the doorway, earning a grateful glance from Flora as he went by her. The pudgy man was one of the last to leave, and he was one of those who always had to get in a final word.

"You haven't heard the end of this. We're respectable folk, and we don't approve of gunplay and such. I'd advise you to leave."

"And if I don't?" Fargo challenged him.

Another man spoke up. "Sheathe your horns, stranger. You can't blame us for wanting you gone. From what I gather, twice now someone has tried to buck you out in gunsmoke. Who's to say they won't try again? We have our families to think of. We don't care to have our wives or children take a bullet meant for you."

Fargo had to admit the man had a point. "I won't be here much longer."

"Fair enough."

Some dispersed but the rest gathered in a knot across the street, talking in low voices and bestowing looks on Fargo that would wither a cactus. Sighing, he closed the door.

"I don't want you to go," Flora said. She was on the divan, her chin downcast in her hands. "Don't let Miss Henderson and those others influence you. I don't give a damn what they think."

"It's your family we should worry about," Fargo informed her. "I won't have you or your children hurt on my account."

"Would you like a drink? I sure would." Flora went to an oak cabinet and removed a bottle of Scotch. She didn't bother to go for glasses. Opening it, she took a long swallow. "Lord, I needed that."

Boots tromped on the porch. Thinking one of the neighbors had come back, Fargo yanked the door open.

Marshal Fred Withers' hand was poised to knock. His clothes were rumpled, his shirt hanging out of his pants. "I should have known you would be involved," he said, brushing past Fargo. "Flora, are you and the children all right?"

"We're fine, Fred."

"What's this about a gunfight in your kitchen?"

"See for yourself."

Flora downed more Scotch and offered the bottle to Fargo, but he declined. Parting the curtains, he saw the neighbors were still out there, the spinster Miss Henderson blathering on about something or other.

Marshal Withers soon returned. Without asking, he took the bottle and helped himself to a long swig. "What is it about you, mister? Everywhere you go, someone tries to dabble you in gore. Who were those men?"

"I never saw them before," Fargo said.

"Is that a fact?" Withers handed the bottle back to Flora. "I knew you were trouble the moment I laid eyes on you. I told you to leave town but you wouldn't listen. And now look. Three men are dead."

"There are only two," Flora corrected him.

The lawman put his hands on her shoulders. "Brace yourself. About half an hour ago I was roused out of bed by Dennis Hickman. He'd found a body in an alley, slit from ear to ear. Near as I can figure it, the man was murdered on his way home from work." Withers paused. "I hate to be the bearer of bad tidings."

"Who was it, Fred? For God's sake, tell me."

"It was Irish Mike."

4

The smell of hay and horses hung heavy in the air when Skye Fargo woke up. It took a few seconds for him to remember where he was. Sitting up, he gazed at the stalls below the hayloft, then at the wide double doors, both open to let sunlight stream in. There was no sign of the crotchety cuss who owned the stable.

Stretching, Fargo pondered his next move. The marshal had directed him to leave town but he wasn't about to, not until he got to the bottom of the mystery, and discovered the link between the attempts on his life and the murder of Mike O'Shay. Marshal Withers didn't believe it was a coincidence, and neither did he. By all accounts Irish Mike had been widely liked and respected. No one had cause to kill him.

Fargo rose and rolled up his bedding. Climbing down the ladder, he placed it with his saddle, then strolled outside. He had slept much longer than he intended. The sun was hours high in the sky.

"That's far enough."

Fargo turned to see Marshall Withers holding a double-barreled shotgun. On his left were two townsmen armed with rifles. Neither seemed particularly eager about being pressed into service, but they held their rifles steady enough.

"What's this?" Fargo asked. As if he couldn't guess.

"I'm not taking no for an answer this time. You're leaving Silver Flats, either on a saddle or draped over one. Unbuckle your gunbelt and let it drop."

The entire street, Fargo noticed, was deserted. Withers had cleared it so none of the town's sterling citizens would be caught in a potential crossfire. As much as Fargo would like to take the shotgun and break it over the lawman's skull, he held his arms out from his sides to show he wouldn't resist. "You're making a mistake."

"The only mistake I made was not doing this sooner," the marshal said. "Three men would still be alive if I had."

"Two of them were hired guns," Fargo reminded him. "Aren't you the least bit interested in finding out who hired them?"

"I can do that on my own. I don't need your help." Withers stepped away from the stable. "I'm not as worthless as you seem to brand me. Irish Mike was a friend of mine. I aim to see his killer hang." He glanced at the two townsmen. "Lucius, Darren, if he so much as touches his six-shooter, you empty your rifles into him. You hear?"

"Will do," one said.

Fargo was worried they might start firing anyway. They were as nervous as two cats in a room full of rocking chairs, constantly twitching and fingering the triggers of their weapons. Moving slowly, Fargo reached for his gun-belt buckle. He had it almost undone when a handsome bay rounded a corner near the general store and a square-jawed rider in his fifties, wearing a fine brown suit and a white hat, trotted toward the stable.

"Mr. Prescott!" Marshal Withers yelled. "Don't come any closer! We're running this jasper out of town."

Prescott didn't draw rein until he was right on top of them. From the sweat on the bay, it was obvious he had ridden hard to get there. "So I heard, Fred. Which is why I've come. I'd like to speak to him in private, if you don't mind."

Fargo studied the manager of the Silverlode. He wasn't in the habit of judging others by first appearances, but Prescott impressed him favorably. The man had an air of openness and honesty about him.

The request had flustered Marshal Withers. "You can't be serious, George! There have been two attempts on his life. There might be another. It isn't healthy to be anywhere around him."

Dismounting, Prescott gave the reins to one of the townsmen. "I'm afraid I must insist, Fred. He could well be the key to the salvation of our town."

"Sir?"

Prescott pressed a finger against Withers' shotgun, swinging the twin barrels aside. "Trust me. There's no need for this. Leave me alone with him. I'll be fine." Facing Fargo, Prescott held out his hand and introduced himself. "I've just come from Mrs. Flannigan's. I went there first after hearing about the shooting affray last night."

"What do you want to talk about?"

"It's for your ears only." Prescott headed into the stable, then paused. "Fred, I would take it as a personal favor if you would spread the word that Mr. Fargo is a friend of mine. He is to be accorded the same respect and courtesy I would. Will you do that for me?"

"Whatever you want," Withers said, unable to hide his confusion.

The tin star wasn't the only one who was confused. Fargo waited until Prescott had pulled the big doors shut, then remarked, "Friends, are we? I've never set eyes on you before."

"Call it wishful thinking," the most powerful man in Silver Flats responded. He sat down on a bale of straw. "I'm hoping we can be friends because, quite frankly, I can use a friend like you. Someone I can rely on."

"Do you always put your trust in total strangers?"

Prescott chuckled and removed his white hat. "I just had a long talk with Flora Flannigan. She vouches for your integrity, and she is as shrewd a judge of character as they come. I've always held her in the highest esteem. No one was sadder at the loss of her husband. He was a good man, a good worker."

"Do you still believe his death was an accident?"

"I don't know what to believe anymore," George Prescott sadly confided, and ran a hand over his thinning sandy hair. "For the past year or so my life has been a living hell. Ever since Flora's husband died, in fact. It was a harbinger of worse to come. Problems plaguing us at the mine. The last payroll disappearing. And now—" Prescott looked up. "I'm at my wit's end, Mr. Fargo. I feel like someone standing on the brink of a cliff, about to be shoved off. And the only one who can pull me back to safety is you."

Fargo sat down on an adjacent bale. "Tell me more."

Anxiety etched George Prescott's face as he commenced. "The Silverlode Mine sits on one of the richest veins of silver in the country, maybe the world. Yet, ironically, the mine is about to go under. If we can't operate at a profit, the consortium backing us will pull out. The Silverlode will shut down and Silver Flats will become yet another ghost town. Hundreds of people will be without jobs. Scores of families will have to start over."

"Go on," Fargo said.

"There have been half a dozen cave-ins since the one that claimed Flynn Flannigan's life. Never in a main tunnel. Never involving more loss of life. But each one has cost us thousands of dollars in extra wages to have the shafts cleared, and in silver revenue lost." Prescott set his hat on his knee. "There have been dozens of strange mishaps. Accidents that shouldn't happen. Ore carts breaking down. New ropes fraying. Tools vanishing."

"And the payroll?"

"It's sent from St. Louis. The last one was in a special locked strongbox on the stage, just like always. But somewhere along the way it up and disappeared."

"An entire strongbox?" Fargo said skeptically. He was familiar with how big and heavy they were. A thief couldn't just throw one over a shoulder and jog off with it.

"The driver and the guard swore they never let it out of their sight for more than a few minutes. My assistant,

Luther Keller, was on that stage and vouches for them." Prescott took a white handkerchief from an inside pocket and mopped his brow. "It's quite clear someone is trying to sabotage the Silverlode. What they hope to gain is beyond me, because even if they shut us down completely they still can't mine the silver on their own, not so long as the consortium owns the mining rights."

"Do you have any idea who it might be?" Fargo did himself, but he wasn't ready to share the information just yet.

"None at all," Prescott said forlornly. "And if I don't turn things around in less than a month, the Silverlode will close."

"Irish Mike told me you're expecting more money soon."

"Another payroll, yes. It's due in on the next stage, this very afternoon. Steps have been taken to guarantee its arrival, including extra guards." Prescott frowned. "What worries me is getting the payroll from here to the mine."

"The stage won't take it?"

"No, the stage line stops at Silver Flats. I'm responsible for the last leg. Ordinarily, I take the money up on the company's mud wagon. That's where you come in."

"I do?"

"If the new payroll is stolen, it will be the last straw. The miners will be destitute. Most have been surviving on credit for months." Prescott gestured. "I'd like to hire you, Mr. Fargo," he said hopefully, "to guard the payroll between town and the Silverlode."

"You think I'm up to the job?" Fargo asked.

"You can handle yourself extremely well. You proved that last night when those men broke into Mrs. Flannigan's house. As I mentioned, she swears by your integrity. And there's one more reason." Prescott was practically begging with his eyes. "There's no one else I can depend on."

Fargo had a thought. "If you're worried about the strongbox being stolen, why not keep it in town and pay your men when they come down for the weekend?"

"And have my employers think I can't perform my job adequately? No, we've always paid the men at the mine. It's just how things are done."

Fargo mulled it over. "I don't usually hire out my gun," he noted. "For the most part I make my living as a scout and a guide."

"But there's no denying that your skill with a six-gun is exceptional," Prescott countered, "and your courage is exceptional." He put his hat back on. "I'll have six other guards, men from the mine, riding point and flank. I'll be there, too, in the wagon. All you have to do is sit on the strongbox for twenty miles."

Prescott made it sound easy enough but Fargo wasn't deceived. Reaching the mine safely would take some careful planning.

"As an added incentive, I'm willing to pay you a thousand dollars out of my own pocket for your efforts. It's worth that much to me to insure the payroll arrives."

Fargo imagined five grinning children at the rail of a churning riverboat on its way down the Missouri River, bound for the wonders of St. Louis. "Make it twelve hundred dollars and we have a deal."

George Prescott thrust out his hand. "Agreed. The stage is due in at four this afternoon. I'll expect you at the stage station to greet it. From then until we reach the Silverlode, the strongbox is your responsibility. If there's anything you need, anything you want done, just say so."

After they shook, and Prescott opened one of the big doors. "I can't thank you enough," he said in parting. "The miners' livelihood isn't the only thing at stake. My own position is in grave jeopardy. The consortium I work for isn't pleased by all the accidents and delays. They hold me personally accountable. If I fail to deliver, I'll be fired, and my reputation will be ruined. I'll never be able to find work at another mine."

"We'll get the money through," Fargo vowed. But would they? If Luther Keller was behind all the problems Prescott was having, he would know about the money due in and take certain steps to prevent it from reaching its destination.

Fargo strolled on out. The wide blue sky was clear of clouds. Silver Flats was bathed in a golden sheen, but under the picturesque surface lurked a viper waiting to strike, a devious sidewinder who had the upper hand because only he knew when and where the next attack would take place.

The skin at the nape of Fargo's neck prickled as he walked down the street. He couldn't shake the nagging sensation that he was being watched from behind every curtain and drape. Irish Mike's curtain was closed. A sign on the door stated that the proprietor had met an untimely end and the saloon would stay closed for the foreseeable future.

A boot scraped behind him. Fargo rotated on the balls of his feet, his hand close to the Colt, but it was only Fred Withers.

"I don't know how you did it, mister."

"Did what, Marshal?"

"Convinced George Prescott to let you ride shotgun on the payroll. He just told me. I tried to talk him out of it but he wouldn't listen." Withers carried a scattergun in the crook of an elbow. "I think he's making a mistake, trusting you. I still believe it's best for the whole town if we run you out."

Fargo would like to see him try. He was growing tired of the man's bullheadedness.

"But Mr. Prescott wants you left alone, and since I was elected largely through his backing, I can't rightly go against his wishes. I'll be keeping my eyes on you, though, Fargo. You won't be able to visit an outhouse without my knowing it."

The lawman clomped off. Fargo slanted across the street to the only other public eatery, Mabel's Cookery. Mabel turned out to be a grizzled old man with a belly the size of a keg and the disposition of a riled grizzly. Most of the tables were filled, mainly with women enjoying tea or coffee.

Their lively chatter died the instant Fargo entered the eatery. He took a corner seat at an empty table.

Wearing an apron smeared with grease and food stains, the grizzled old man came over. "The special of the day is elk meat, potatoes, and fresh bread. Coffee is extra but you can have as much as you want."

"Do you have anything else?" Fargo asked, hoping for some ham and eggs with buttered toast and jam.

"What do you have against elk meat?"

"I like it just fine," Fargo conceded. "But what if a customer is hungry for something else?"

"Then that customer can go out and grub for roots, for all I care," the man gruffly responded. "The special of the day also happens to be the *only* meal of the day. So quit wasting my time and order."

The meal was surprisingly delicious, the meat flavored with seasoning, the potatoes covered in cheese, the bread so hot and tasty Fargo almost devoured a whole loaf at one sitting. On top of that, the coffee was dark and strong, potent enough to jolt one right out of their seat.

Fargo paid no heed to the curious stares directed his way. He was almost done when the tiny bell above the door jangled and in came Flora Flannigan. She had on a plain everyday dress and carried a handbag. Spotting Fargo, she made a beeline for his table.

"I've been hunting all over for you, handsome."

Fargo pulled out a chair for her, then sat back down. The assembled biddy hens were in a tizzy, whispering and pointing. He had half a mind to kiss Flora full on the lips to really give them something to gossip about.

She bent closer. "I wish you had stayed last night. The kids were disappointed you weren't there when they got up."

"That's nice of them," Fargo said. But under no circumstances would he put the family in any more danger than he already had.

"Mr. Prescott came by. He asked a lot of questions about you and said he was going to look you up."

"He did," Fargo said. "I agreed to help him out." He refrained from saying why he had agreed.

"Then you'll be in town for one more night?" Flora brightened. "The children and I would be delighted if you'd come for supper again. And you're more than welcome to stay over. It's unlikely whoever sent those men will try anything."

Fargo disagreed. "I can't."

"Please, Skye." Flora set the other women buzzing by resting her hand on his. "I thoroughly enjoy your company. So does my brood. One night more is all I'm asking."

"No." Fargo was stung by the hurt in her eyes. But she was asking a lot more than she let on, and they both knew it.

"That's your final say on the subject?"

"I'm afraid so." Fargo averted his gaze.

"Well, that's plain enough." Flora let out a long sigh. "In that case, I should be off. I need to find a new job as soon as possible. Irish Mike's death has put me in a bind. There's barely enough money in the cookie jar to last a couple of weeks."

"I have a few extra dollars—" Fargo began.

"Thank you kindly, but no. A Flannigan doesn't accept handouts. We work for our keep. I'm sure the good Lord will provide. He hasn't let us down yet." Standing, Flora fussed with her handbag a moment. "I guess I shouldn't have gotten my hopes up, should I? You never made any false promises."

"One day the right man will come along. In St. Louis you'll have them lining up for the honor of your company."

"You're a sweet liar," Flora said, and left.

The buzzing grew louder. Resentment formed a knot in Fargo's gut. He almost jumped to his feet and roared, "Quit talking about her behind her back! She's worth more than any ten of you combined!" Instead, he paid for his meal and stalked out. Wheeling to the left, he nearly collided with a big man in a suit and bowler hat.

"Watch where you're going," Luther Keller snapped, then jerked his head back as if he had been punched. "Oh! It's you."

"Surprised I'm still alive?" Fargo said. Standing beyond Keller was the swarthy gunman, Harvey. "I see you have your shadow along. Does he hold your handkerchief for you when you blow your nose, too?"

The gun shark took a step forward but Keller held out his arm, stopping him. "I wouldn't antagonize Harvey, were I you. He's killed men for less."

"By shooting them from rooftops?"

Both men colored, the gunman's lips drawing back from his teeth in a soundless snarl. Luther Keller regained his composure and responded. "That's not an accusation, by any chance, is it, Mr. Fargo? Because I can produce half a dozen men who will swear that Harvey was nowhere near the assayer's office when the attempt on your life was made."

"It's amazing what money will buy, huh?"

Keller wasn't the least bit amused. "I find that I despise you more today than I did yesterday, which I didn't think was possible. But I'm a reasonable man, Mr. Fargo. My advice to you is to saddle up and ride out while you still can. You have involved yourself in matters beyond your ability to remedy."

"That's not a threat, is it?" Fargo mimicked him.

"No, not at all. Consider it more in the way of a friendly warning. You're like an aspen caught in the path of a rock slide. There's nothing you can do to stop it. And once it reaches you, it will crush you like a twig." Smirking, Keller moved on by. "Should you decide to leave, I'll be more than happy to buy whatever supplies you need and give you a little spending money to get you on your way."

"There is one thing you can do for me," Fargo said.

"Oh?"

"Tell me why you had Irish Mike killed. Was it because he heard me mention Billy Pardee? Were you covering your tracks?"

Luther Keller's mouth creased in a wicked smile. "Why, Mr. Fargo, I have no idea what you're talking about. I thought quite highly of Mike O'Shay." Tapping his bowler, he slid into the restaurant, the dark gunman glued to his side.

Stewing, Fargo made for the stable. Down the street Marshall Withers was leaning against a post, watching him closely. Fargo contemplated telling the lawman about his conversation with Keller, but didn't waste his breath. Withers would never believe him.

The hours dragged by. To pass the time, Fargo brushed the Ovaro and gave it some oats, then sat on a bench in front of the stable, the Henry across his lap. He had a clear view of the main street and the front of all the roofs. No one could sneak up on him or try to pick him off without being seen. No one tried, though. Nor did any of the town's upright citizens come anywhere near him. The women and few men going about their daily business gave the stable a wide berth. They wanted nothing to do with the stranger who had only brought more trouble to their quiet town.

Fargo was glad when he finally heard the pounding of hooves, heralding the arrival of the stage. It rolled on down the street at a brisk clip, sweeping past him toward the stage station. The coach brimmed with armed guards, including two on top. Rifle barrels poked from every window like the jutting quills of a porcupine.

George Prescott and Luther Keller emerged from the station to greet it as curious folk stepped out from buildings for a look-see. In a town like Silver Flats, where little else broke the monotony of the daily routine, the appearance of the stage was a major event.

A large crowd had gathered around by the time Fargo got there. He shouldered through them, not giving a damn whose feathers he ruffled. The strongbox had been deposited on the boardwalk and the guards were standing around awaiting instructions.

Luther Keller turned to George Prescott. "I say we lock it in the office overnight and post a man to keep watch. It should be safe enough until morning."

"One man won't be enough," Prescott said.

Fargo stepped forward. "He will if he's the only one who knows where the money is." Moving onto the boardwalk, he gave the strongbox a thump with the Henry's stock. "Take the money, put it in saddlebags, and turn it over to me."

Keller was incredulous. "Do *what*? You honestly expect us to turn over fifteen thousand dollars to a saddle tramp?"

No one had time to react to what occurred next. In two bounds Fargo reached Keller and drove the Henry into the pit of his abdomen. Keller folded like an accordion, swearing furiously, while Harvey shifted his hand toward the ivory grips of his Smith & Wesson. Fargo only had to move his wrist and the Henry's muzzle was against Harvey's side. "Go ahead. I'd like nothing better than to pay you back for yesterday."

George Prescott was bewildered. "Mr. Fargo! What's the meaning of this? I only hired you to guard the money from here to the mine, not overnight."

Fargo backed up next to him. "Don't you want the payroll to reach the Silverlode?"

"Of course, but—"

"Then you'll turn it over to me for safekeeping." Fargo motioned at the stage station. "Leave it there and you'll never see it again. Post all the men you want and it won't make a lick of difference."

A hand fell on Fargo's shoulder and he spun, his thumb curling back the Henry's hammer. Again, Fargo turned to see the cold, glaring eyes of Marshal Fred Withers.

"I saw what you just did. You had no call to hit Mr. Keller. You're under arrest for assault."

Fargo moved to lash into the marshal, but Prescott

moved between them. "Please, Fred, overlook his indiscretion. We need this man, more than you realize." Taking Fargo by the sleeve, Prescott pulled him around to the other side of the stage. "What do you know that I don't? Why did you strike Luther? Do you really think you should keep the payroll until morning?"

"Sometime tomorrow I expect you'll know as much as I do. As for Keller, he made the mistake of prodding me once too often."

"And the money?"

Fargo raised his voice on purpose. "If you keep it in the stage station, everyone in town will know where it is. Including the person trying to close down the mine."

"I see your point. It's like inviting a fox to raid the chicken coop. But is it any wiser for you to have sole responsibility?"

"No one can steal it from me if they don't know where to find me."

"You'll hide out somewhere? An excellent idea, but you're putting your life at great risk. Whoever is behind all this will have his paid killers hunt you down."

"Let them try," Fargo declared, hoping he wouldn't regret his words from the grave.

5

From the top of a hill a mile to the southwest of Silver
Flats, Skye Fargo intently watched the bobbing lantern
light that had been following him for the past thirty minutes. Someone was hunting him. Or, rather, hunting the
money they thought was crammed into the extra saddlebags
tied on the Ovaro. How they were doing it was a mystery,
because even with a lantern, tracking at night was a slow,
painstaking chore. Yet whoever was after him had glued
themselves to his trail and not lost it once.

What made it all the more remarkable was that Fargo had
taken steps to confuse would-be pursuers. He had doubled
back. He had used branches to brush out his tracks. He had
resorted to every trick he knew. But it wasn't enough.

The moon hung above the eastern horizon in all its sil-
very glory. Ghostly clouds floated on high, borne by a stiff
breeze. From the mountains at Fargo's back wafted the stri-
dent yipping of coyotes and from higher up, the eerie howling of wolves on the prowl.

Fargo was more concerned about the two-legged variety
of scavenger below. He had left Silver Flats before dark,
over Luther Keller's fierce objections. Keller had been
livid, incensed that George Prescott had turned the payroll
over to him and even more outraged that Prescott had allowed him to leave town with it.

Luther Keller wasn't the only one who had objected.
Marshal Fred Withers had told Prescott to his face that he
was making the biggest mistake of his life. Several promi-

nent townsmen complained bitterly that Fargo couldn't be trusted. Most everyone was of the opinion that Prescott had doomed the town to extinction.

What Luther Keller didn't know—and what no one else in Silver Flats knew—was that the money was snug in the stage station's safe. Prescott had shooed everyone out of the building before they supposedly switched the payroll from the strongbox to the saddlebags.

Indeed, Prescott had been all set to do just that until Fargo explained the ruse he had in mind. Let everyone think he had the money. Let whoever wanted it scurry around like rats trying to find him. The money would be safe, right where it should be.

Fargo's extra saddlebags contained periodicals and flyers that were lying around the stage office, along with a few rags for good measure. Fargo had carried them out, strapped them on, then immediately lit a shuck for the foothills.

The word that Fargo had the payroll was all over Silver Flats soon enough. But whoever was after him now had started out immediately after he left, which meant it had to be someone who was there when the supposed switch took place.

Cradling the Henry, Fargo tried to tell how many were after him but the lantern was still too far off. He saw the circle of light bob toward the ground and swing from side to side, then rise as the man holding it climbed back into the saddle. It made Fargo smile to think of how mad they would be if they knew they were being led on a useless chase.

After ten minutes, Fargo forked leather and resumed riding. At the base of the hill he reined to the north, toward rugged, broken country that would tax the trackers even more. He rode at a leisurely pace. There was no hurry, he thought. Not with the lead he had. All he had to do was maintain it, and then circle back to town.

Another howl wavered on the wind, courtesy of the wolf pack abroad in the thick timber up near the snow line. It stirred a yearning in Fargo to shed civilization and return to the wilderness. But he couldn't, not yet, not with George Prescott and the entire town of Silver Flats depending on him.

Fargo traveled a quarter of a mile, then thought to glance over his shoulder. He was startled to see his pursuers had cut the distance by half. Fargo could discern shadowy riders surrounding the man with the lantern, who had dismounted again. There were other shapes, too, smaller, four-legged figures milling close to the lantern, their noses to the ground.

Insight spurred Fargo into bringing the stallion to a gallop. Simultaneously, the night was pierced by new howls. Only these weren't the lonesome wails of wolves or coyotes. These were the throaty bays of hunting dogs in full chorus.

Fargo hadn't anticipated this. The dogs had the Ovaro's scent, so shaking his pursuers would be next to impossible. Angling up onto a heavily forested slope, he threaded through the pines and firs, avoiding deadfalls and tangles. He had to think of a means to slow the dogs down or stop them altogether.

The hounds' baying grew louder. The lantern was moving rapidly, bouncing up and down as it would be if the man holding it were riding at a trot.

Fargo came to a sixty-yard belt of charred trees, the result of a lightning strike and a subsequent fire. Most of them had long since fallen over. He had to pick his way with care to avoid injury to the pinto. Once on the far side, he climbed down and yanked the Henry from its scabbard.

It wasn't long before his pursuers reached the bottom of the slope, the lantern jiggling and swaying on top of the horse. The hounds had stopped baying, perhaps silenced by their owner. But as the riders neared the belt of charred trees, one uttered a throaty howl.

Fargo counted eight mounted men, possibly more. Sitting down, he propped his elbows on his legs and steadied the Henry. At that range, the lantern appeared no larger than an apple, and its constant motion added to the difficulty of a successful shot. Nevertheless, Fargo centered the sights on it.

The hounds suddenly went into a frenzy. The scent told them they were close to their quarry, and they were letting their masters know.

After another moment, the riders reined up. The one holding the lantern climbed down to examine the ground. He sank onto his knees, swinging the lantern from side to side, then lowered it.

Fargo guessed the man was studying the Ovaro's tracks. He levered a round into the chamber, sucked in a deep breath, and stayed perfectly still as his forefinger curled around the trigger. The lantern hadn't moved. His finger stroked the trigger crisply, cleanly, the booming retort rolling off down the foothills toward the distant plain.

At the blast, the ball of light dissolved in a shower of sparks and flame. Oaths and yells rent the night, along with the whinnies of frightened, prancing horses and the barking of the dogs. A few shots cracked but they came nowhere near Fargo. The men were firing blind, out of fear.

"Stop it!" someone thundered. "Quit your damn shooting!"

Fargo was on the move again before they brought their animals under control. He climbed to the crest, paralleled it to the north, and ventured down a steep incline into a dry wash that ran from east to west. It was an ideal place to start heading for town without being spotted. But as he tapped his spurs against the pinto, more deep howls erupted above him.

A glance showed Fargo four lithe shapes loping eagerly down the hill. The hounds had been unleashed! He rode faster, but the dogs had spied him and were making enough racket to be heard clear back in Silver Flats. The scrabble of their claws on stone alerted Fargo that they had already reached the wash, and he looked back again.

They were strung out in single file, the biggest of the four in the lead, his cries echoing off the low wash walls. Each was over two feet high at the shoulders and had to weigh upward of one hundred pounds, with flaring nostrils and long, floppy ears.

Fargo would rather elude them than shoot them. They were only doing what they had been trained to do. But they were amazingly swift, able to keep up with the stallion in the confines of the winding wash. He needed open space to outdistance them. But leaving the wash wouldn't help much. Woodland loomed on both sides, and in dense forest the quick hounds would easily overtake him.

Fargo drew his Colt, reckoning he might drive them off with a few shots. As the big lead dog hurtled around a bend, he fired twice, zinging slugs off a boulder just in front of the racing hound. But it had no more effect than peas from a pea shooter. The dogs never broke stride, never slowed. Losing them was going to take some doing. Fargo shoved the Colt under his belt and knuckled down to the task of riding hell-bent for leather, a perilous undertaking at any time, but doubly so in the dark.

Fargo could hear the heavy breathing of the lead hound on the Ovaro's heels. The dogs were sprinting all out, putting on a burst of speed in a last-ditch attempt to catch him. Another precarious turn forced Fargo to slow a trifle, which was all the foremost dog needed.

Teeth gnashed, grinding like steel on flint. The brute was trying to bite into the stallion's rear legs. Should it succeed, and hamstring the Ovaro, Fargo might be forced to put the stallion down. He'd rather cut off his own arm.

Fargo pointed the Colt just as the brute lunged for another try. His shot smashed into the hound's forehead and the dog tumbled in a whirl of flailing legs.

The other three veered around their fallen leader, the one now at the forefront soon doing exactly as the first had done, fiercely nipping at the Ovaro's legs. They swept around a turn, and once on a straight stretch, Fargo took aim. But the stallion stopped the second hound on its own. Just as the dog rushed in close to bite, snarling viciously, a flashing kick from a heavy hoof caught it flush in the face.

The sledgehammer impact sent the canine crashing backward. That left two, and neither showed any sign of giving up.

They weren't the only problem Fargo faced. Shooting out the lantern had been a mistake. It had alerted his pursuers he was close by, which was why they had unleashed the pack. Now the gunmen were no doubt close behind, guided by the din.

Fargo had to dispose of the dogs before the riders caught up. He banged a shot at the third one but missed, as the Ovaro had careened sideways to avoid a boulder. He sighted carefully, but again a boulder caused the pinto to veer.

The remaining dogs were howling madly to let their masters know where they were, just as they would do if they were after a raccoon, a fox, or a bear. The racket was unnerving.

Yet another bend appeared. The Ovaro went around it at a full gallop—and almost collided with a pine. Hauling on the reins, Fargo saved himself from disaster, then had to cut in the other direction when more trees hove out of the night. The dry wash had come to an end. He was in a tract of trees, their trunks rearing on all sides like spectral sentinels. If not for the pale light of the moon, he'd never have seen them in time.

Fargo slowed, enabling the bloodhounds to quickly close the gap. Suddenly a dog was on either side, trying to tear at the pinto. He couldn't concentrate on them and the trees at the same time. He had to slow even more, but as he did, he shifted and fired into the dog on the left. Though he hit it, the husky bloodhound bared its fangs and launched itself at the stallion's belly. Fargo had to empty his Colt into the dog's torso in order to put it down for good.

Without warning, the Ovaro came to a sliding halt, all on its own. Fargo looked up and saw a deadfall in their path.

The pinto began to swerve around it, the last hound snapping at its legs. In a matter of seconds, those razor teeth would connect.

Fargo couldn't let that happen. He flung himself from the saddle. The hound was so intent on bringing the Ovaro down, it didn't notice the large, broad-shouldered man flying toward it. Fargo landed on top of the dog, beating it to the earth. He clubbed at its head and felt a couple of blows connect, but then it slipped free, raking his shin with its claws as it did.

The hound backed up a few steps and crouched. Bristling, it rumbled deep in its barrel chest.

Quickly, Fargo switched the Colt from his right hand to his left and dropped his right arm to his boot. With a savage yip, the bloodhound pounced, rushing in low and incredibly fast. Fargo made no attempt to leap out of the way. In the blink of an eye the animal was on him, relying on its brute strength and dazzling speed to prevail. But the dog didn't know about Fargo's ace in the hole—the Arkansas toothpick in his right boot.

Fargo whisked the knife from its sheath and thrust upward, the cold steel shearing into the hound's chest just as the dog leaped. Both of them went down, the dog biting and clawing, Fargo slicing the blade lower. Warm, sticky blood spread over his hand and down his arm. The hound gave a violent wrench, almost tearing the toothpick from his grasp, but Fargo held on, driving it steadily lower, carving through flesh like a hot knife through tallow.

The bloodhound thrashed a few times, organs spilling from its abdominal cavity. Then it was still.

Shoving the dead weight away, Fargo slowly rose. He was winded and bruised and had cuts on his legs and arms. Blood caked his right sleeve. His shirt was soaked where the mongrel's innards had spilled over him, giving off a foul reek.

"Too close, " Fargo said softly. "Much too close." Wiping the toothpick clean on the hound's coat, he slid it back into his ankle sheath.

Clattering hooves reminded him of the men anxious to bury him. Fargo dashed to the Ovaro. It was wide-eyed, its nostrils flaring, feet prancing nervously. He snagged the saddle horn and pulled himself up, then reined to the left to maneuver around the deadfall.

And none too soon. His pursuers galloped around the last bend in the wash and instantly drew rein, stopping less than twenty yards off.

"The dogs have stopped howling!" one man declared.

"What could have happened?" asked another.

"What the hell do you think, you peckerwood," snapped a short figure in a narrow-brimmed hat. "He's done killed them."

"The boss won't be too happy, Pardee," said a fourth. "He paid a lot of money for those mangy critters."

"What about the jasper we're after?" someone else wanted to know. "Do we give up or go on?"

Fargo moved off slowly. They hadn't spotted him yet, and with a little luck they wouldn't. In addition to Billy Pardee, he'd recognized Decker's voice, Billy's friend with the scarred cheek. That meant the tall hardcase with the cold eyes must be along, too.

"The boss will blister our ears if we just give up," Pardee said. "Spread out in pairs, boys. If you spot him, fire some shots and the rest of us will come a-runnin'. There are eleven of us and only one of him. He'll be maggot bait before mornin'."

"Says you," responded another voice Fargo recognized, that of the scarecrow from Flora's. "He's no greenhorn. And he's lightning on the draw."

Billy Pardee snickered. "Sounds to me as if you're a mite scared, Calhoun. Maybe you should tuck your tail between your skinny legs and ride on back to town. Let us men handle this."

"Quit your bickering," another gunman declared. "I swear, the two of you spat like cats and dogs."

"That's because they both want to be Keller's straw boss," said someone else. "They're each trying to outdo the other."

Fargo would soon be out of earshot. They were so busy arguing, he would get clean away. But even as the thought crossed his mind, the stallion moved forward and was bathed by a random beam of moonlight through the trees. He reined aside but the harm had been done.

"Look! There he is!"

"After him, you lunkheads!" Billy Pardee shouted.

"We have him now!" Calhoun said.

Whooping and hollering, the gun sharks sped into the pines. They crashed through the undergrowth, breaking limbs and crushing brush, making more noise than the braying bloodhounds had. Shots boomed out.

Fargo fled deeper into the woodland, bent low to make a smaller target of himself. To the gunmen, this was sport, the result preordained. They were bound to win with odds so heavily in their favor.

To discourage them, Fargo knew he must shoot one or two. But his Colt was empty and he couldn't handle the reins and use the rifle at the same time, not with so many obstacles to avoid. So he did the only thing he could: he raced for his life.

"Spread out, boys!" Pardee bawled. "Don't let him flank us!"

Fargo swung wide of a stand of tightly packed firs. Another gun boomed, louder than the rest, the unmistakable discharge of a rifle. One of the killers was using his head. Fargo bent lower as the rifle thundered again and he heard the angry swarm of lead directly overhead.

"Shoot the pinto! Shoot the pinto!"

"I'm trying, you idiot!"

It was what Fargo dreaded most. A thicket served to screen the stallion for a short distance, but once he was beyond it the woodland began to thin out. He had been traveling downhill since leaving the dry wash, and he had a hunch he would soon reach open ground. When that happened, the gunmen would have no problem picking him off.

More and more shots shattered the darkness, most wide of their mark. Several came uncomfortably near, though, one smacking into the bole of a tree only an arm's length from Fargo's head. He reined to the left, then to the right, never traveling in a straight line for more than fifteen or twenty yards. But he knew he was only delaying the inevitable.

Fargo glimpsed a patch of clear ground ahead. He had to slow the gunmen down, or else. Taking a gamble, he drew rein and wheeled the Ovaro. Yanking out the Henry, he hiked it to his shoulder. Pardee's bunch had fanned out and were closing rapidly, each hell-bent to be the one to bring him down. Pumping the lever, Fargo took a hasty bead on one of the nearest and fired. A scream and a whinny greeted the retort. Instantly Fargo injected a new round into the chamber and squeezed the trigger. A second gunman fell.

It brought the rest to a stop. They exchanged shouts. One of them was screeching, "I'm hit! I'm hit!"

Not wasting a second, Fargo brought the stallion around and applied his spurs. He was out of the trees before another shot resounded. The open grassland extended for over half a mile, and the lights of Silver Flats twinkled in the distance. Reaching the town unseen was out of the question. He cut to the north, thinking to loop into the woods again before the gunmen emerged.

Out of nowhere, a gully materialized. It wasn't long or deep, no more than twenty feet from end to end and not much higher than the Ovaro, but it gave Fargo an idea. He rode down into it and reined to a halt.

Vaulting off the pinto, Fargo gripped the bridle with one hand and tugged while lightly smacking his other palm against the stallion's foreleg. It was a trick Fargo had taught the Ovaro, having picked it up from the wily Comanches, the best horsemen on the southern plains. The Ovaro balked a bit, then sank down onto its side. Patting the pinto's neck, Fargo whispered, "Good boy." Then he ran up to the gully's rim and flattened himself on the edge.

Out of the forest trotted six of the hired guns. Billy Pardee was among them, and when he raised his arm, they halted.

"Where the hell did he get to?" the young Texan demanded.

Decker rubbed his scarred cheek. "Don't this beat all. He couldn't have gone very far. Maybe he slipped back into the trees."

"We'd have seen him," Calhoun added.

"Or heard him," said the tall Texan with the icy eyes.

Billy rose in his stirrups. "Well, he sure as shootin' has to be *somewhere*. While Rafe and Garvey tend to Foster, we'll scour the area. Keep your eyes skinned and your six-shooters cocked."

Pardee and Decker rode to the east. Calhoun and the Texan bore to the south. The fifth cantered northward along the tree line while the last gunman roved in a northwesterly direction—toward the gully.

Fargo had his chin resting on the ground, the Henry ready for use. High grass concealed him for now, but once the gunman was close enough, he'd be able to see Fargo.

A nickel-plated pistol glistened dully in the hair-trigger artist's hand, and another was on his left hip. Evidently he fancied himself a two-gun man, a rarity in these parts.

"Anything, Po?" called out the rider at the tree line.

"No trace of the hombre, Zeb," Po answered. His sorrel plodded along with its head hung low, weary from the long chase.

"You'd think he was a ghost, the way he vanished," Zeb said. "Between you and me, I'd fight shy of this outfit right this minute if not for the money Keller promised us. A thousand dollars is more than I can earn in three years."

For most men, that much money was a small fortune. Small wonder, Fargo mused, that Keller had been able to persuade so many gunmen to back him.

"I hear you, pard," Po was saying. "My share will buy me some prime grazing land down Durango way and enough cattle to start my own ranch."

"Hell. Save your money and steal the cows," Zeb suggested.

Po glanced at him. "Are you loco? And have my neighbors accuse me of using a running iron? Once I start on the straight and narrow, I aim to stay on it. I've had enough of the owlhoot trail to last me a lifetime."

The two-gun hardcase was close enough to the gully for Fargo to bean him with a rock. But Fargo didn't move. He scarcely breathed.

The sorrel's head rose and the horse looked toward where Fargo lay. The Trailsman tensed, suspecting it had caught his scent, or more likely the Ovaro's. But the sorrel didn't nicker or do anything else to give him away.

Po reined to the east. "If you ask me, that gent in buckskins is long gone," he said quietly to his mount. "This is a waste of time. But I'm being paid to do as the boss wants, so I reckon we'll wear your horseshoes down a little more before we call it quits for the night."

Horse and rider passed within twenty feet of the gully, yet Po never spotted it. He was gazing into the distance, not at the ground around him. Soon both faded into the darkness. Not long after, the night swallowed Zeb, too.

Fargo's gambit had worked. He waited several minutes, and when none of the outlaws reappeared, he brought the Ovaro to its feet and climbed onto the hurricane deck. Moving to the west end of the gully, he rose high enough in the stirrups to scan the immediate vicinity. No gunmen were anywhere to be seen.

Fargo rode up and out at a walk and crossed toward the forest. He didn't want to draw attention by moving any faster. No shouts broke the stillness, and no lead was thrown his way.

With gunmen to the east, south, and north, Fargo rode in the one direction they were least likely to guess he would take: due west, away from town. After covering half a mile, he trotted southward, ultimately bearing east again when he was confident he had gone far enough.

Fargo reached Silver Flats along about two in the morning. An alley brought him to the rear of the stage station. After he rapped on the door, it was jerked open.

George Prescott smiled warmly. "Your ploy worked? I was beginning to think it hadn't. You told me you'd be back by midnight."

"The posse after me were harder to shake than I expected," Fargo said. He walked to a small stove and poured himself a cup of coffee. Guards were positioned at the windows and the front door. The safe, with its invaluable contents, sat behind a large desk.

"Did you get a good look at any of them? Do you know who the mastermind is?"

Fargo took a sip. He still didn't have proof. Accusing Keller would only anger Prescott, who might do something rash. "Let's just say we'll both find out for sure soon enough."

"How soon? By this time tomorrow the payroll will be at the mine. We'll have won. Whoever is behind all the trouble will crawl back under the slimy rock they slithered out from under, and we'll never learn who it was."

Fargo looked at him. Some people were too naive for their own good. "It's a long way from town to the mine."

"But we'll have six guards along, with orders to shoot to kill. I've deliberately spread the news around town to scare off anyone who might try to rob us."

"Six guards or sixteen, it won't matter," Fargo said. "The mastermind, as you call him, won't stop until he gets whatever he's after. No matter how many people he has to kill."

6

Men like Luther Keller prided themselves on how clever they were, and Keller's scheme to shut down the Silverlode Mine was devious. But he was so determined to achieve his goal at any and all costs, he had overlooked a crucial fact.

The money going to the Silverlode Mine totaled over fifteen thousand dollars. Most of it was in bills, but there was also several hundred dollars in coin. The entire payroll couldn't possibly fit in a pair of saddlebags, and even if it did, the weight and bulk of the coins would cause the seams to burst.

Skye Fargo had half expected Luther Keller to realize that, and to deduce he was being tricked. The man was so intent on stealing the money, though, he hadn't stopped to think it out. Also, Keller's hatred of Fargo and his desire to see the Trailsman dead were factors in his hasty ploy.

But there was no tricking Keller this time.

The strongbox was in the mud wagon and the mud wagon was now rolling out of Silver Flats with three guards riding ahead and three behind. Most everyone in town had turned out to see it off. Smiling and waving, they lined both sides of the main street. Their livelihoods, the welfare of their entire families, depended on the wagon reaching the Silverlode safely. Fargo detected more than a hint of anxiety in many of their expressions.

The mud wagon was smaller and lighter than a Concord stage but shared the same general design. It had the standard driver's seat, a rear boot for transporting supplies, and a similar thoroughbrace suspension. Typically, the rear wheels were much larger than the front. Unlike stage-coaches, mud wagons had canvas tops and were built closer to the ground. They were also considerably lighter. As a result, they were able to handle the roughest of trails, roads no stage could negotiate.

Fargo had ridden in a few before. The experience was nothing to crow about. Passengers were constantly jostled back and forth and from side to side. Flies and choking dust were also a constant nuisance because the canvas flaps that covered the windows were about as useful as teats on a bull.

George Prescott insisted on having the flaps rolled up. He wanted to be able to admire the countryside.

Fargo thought it was a mistake. Anyone who wanted to pick them off could see right in. But the thing that upset him the most was the fact Prescott hadn't told him two other passengers were going along, both of whom were better off staying in Silver Flats.

Across from the mine's manager sat a nervous easterner, fresh off yesterday's stage. He had said little since Prescott introduced him as one Percival Porter. A cheap suit and a straw hat showed that whatever he did for a living did not pay exceptionally well. Clutched in his lap was a large square leather carrying case.

Across from Fargo sat someone who interested him a little more. She had reddish hair, pinned up in a bun, clear blue eyes, exquisitely shaped raspberry lips, and a ready smile. In her early twenties, her full lush figure was clothed in a plain white dress. In her lap was a black bag such as the ones doctors used. Her name was Cynthia Howard.

That was all Fargo knew about her, but he would certainly like to know more. His first concern, though, was for her safety, and that of the easterner. As the mud wagon rattled on out of Silver Flats, he turned to the man who had hired him. "I said it before, I'll say it again. It's a mistake to take these two along. You're putting their lives at risk."

Prescott was in surprisingly fine spirits. "A small risk, I should think. With six outriders, plus the driver and the shotgun guard—not to mention you here to protect us, I feel perfectly safe. No one would be foolhardy enough to attack us."

"Besides," the easterner said in a high voice that squeaked more than the mud wagon did, "I have my duty to perform. It's imperative I reach the Silverlode without delay."

"Why is that, Percival?" Fargo asked dryly.

"Call me Percy, please. Only my mother calls me Percival." He patted the carrying case. "These are ledgers. I'm an accountant, sir. In the employ of the Anaheim Consortium. It's my job to audit their varied business enterprises. I'm to go over the Silverlode's book and report back to them as soon as I can."

"That's worth your life?"

Percy tittered. "You exaggerate, surely. Just as everyone exaggerated the perils of making this trip. I was led to believe Indians lurked behind every tree, footpath, and in every alley. But as you can see, I'm hearty and hale and enjoying my adventure immensely."

Fargo looked at the redhead. "What's your reason for wanting to die?"

Cynthia Howard smiled, displaying dazzlingly white teeth. "I should think it would be obvious. I'm a nurse, Mr. Fargo. I visit the Silverlode once a month to treat ailing miners. This happens to be my next scheduled visit."

"You couldn't postpone it a few days?"

"Why should I? I don't share your apprehension. I've ridden up before with a strongbox and nothing ever happened. Why should this time be any different?"

Fargo glanced at the accountant, then back at the nurse. They seemed to think that bad things always happened to others, not to them. It was a common, if peculiar, trait, a misguided assumption that they were somehow special, that they would be spared the hardships and heartaches every one else experienced. He had met many people who were the same way. The worst were those who believed they had a special link to the Almighty, that their Maker would spare them from life's cruelties. They were usually in for a rude awakening.

"When the shooting starts," Fargo said, "I want both of you to keep low and do exactly as I say."

"My, my," Cynthia said. "You certainly have a flair for the melodramatic."

"No, I have a flair for the practical," Fargo countered.

George Prescott cleared his throat. "Please. There's no call to needlessly scare her. We have enough men and rifles to drive off a small army."

"I can also be of help," Percy said. Reaching under his jacket, he held out a two-barrel derringer with gutta-percha grips. "I bought this in New Orleans a couple of years ago. The man who sold it to me said it would stop a charging buffalo."

It was a .22-caliber Marston. Fargo doubted very much the accountant could stop a rabbit, let alone anything bigger. All he said, though, was, "Have you had much practice with that thing?"

Percy grinned. "Once I set up a bottle and practiced for an hour. I hit it four times, too. The bullets made the cutest little holes."

Fargo gazed out the wagon to keep from laughing. He was annoyed at Prescott for saddling him with the two innocents, one of them a woman, no less. Both would be fortunate to see the next dawn. He was annoyed at himself, too, for not insisting more strongly that they stay in town. He should have held the Henry against Prescott's head and *made* him give in.

"I'm armed as well," Cynthia said.

Fargo was afraid to ask. "You are?"

Cynthia pulled a six-inch hairpin from her bun. "I can put a man's eyes out with this, or worse."

Fargo could see it now. If they were jumped by Keller's bunch, he'd ask Billy Pardee to step up to the mud wagon so the nurse could bury her weapon in Pardee's groin, while the rest of the gunmen would promptly ride off in stark fear. He let out with a long sigh.

"Is something the matter?" Cynthia asked.

"Nothing a bottle of whiskey wouldn't cure."

They were crossing the grassland at a brisk clip. Soon enough they reached the foothills, and the driver was still able to push the six-horse team at twice the speed a stage-coach would be able to navigate in this terrain. The road was fairly wide, the turns gradual, the grades not too terribly steep.

All that changed drastically once they came to the mountains.

The road became a hazardous winding ribbon, curving steadily upward, often at such a steep grade that Cynthia and Percy had to hold on to the sides to keep from being pitched from the front seat. The driver was constantly cracking his whip and bawling to his team, "Get along, there! Get along!"

Cynthia rarely spoke. From time to time Fargo caught her studying him. Percy prattled on about the exciting life of an accountant, about the cities he had been to, the colorful people he had met, the sights he had seen. He probably would have prattled all the way to the mine, but once the mud wagon started up into the Rockies, they were all constantly swaying and bouncing, and Percy shut up and turned a sickly hue.

A new jolt caused Percy to swallow hard, then bleat, "Is the rest of our journey going to be this bad? I'm afraid my stomach doesn't have the iron constitution I thought it did."

"It will get a lot rougher, I'm sorry to say," Prescott informed him. "Close eyes and try not to dwell on it."

"I'll try."

Fargo continually scanned the slopes on the south side. The higher the wagon climbed, the steeper those slopes became. Some were heavily forested, others were dotted with massive boulders and scrub. Snatches of conversation between the driver and the shotgun guard drifted down, some-thing about an elk hunt the two planned to go on soon.

The outriders were all business, though. Those in front and in back rode with their rifles out, always vigilant. When the mud wagon came to a spot where a small tree had fallen across the road, four of the riders ringed the wagon while the other two tied a rope to the tree and dragged it out of the way.

George Prescott's confidence was growing by leaps and bounds. Three hours out of Silver Flats he consulted his watch and smiled. "We're past the midway point and noth-ing has happened."

"We still have seven or eight miles to go," Fargo noted. And they would be the worst miles, for they were traveling a lot slower, and would thus be easier to ambush.

"I admire your devotion to your job," Prescott said, "but you can relax. If the bandits haven't struck by now, I doubt they will."

The mud wagon suddenly gave a violent lurch. Leaning out, Fargo saw that it had hit a pothole. Ahead reared a nar-row gorge, its bottom plunged in shadow. It was an ideal site to be bushwhacked. He beckoned to the riders behind the wagon, who moved in closer. They didn't like this sce-nario any better than he did, and they craned their necks to scour the heights.

Percy was holding his stomach and puffing out his cheeks. "I don't feel very well," he said, snatching the nurse's wrist. "Isn't there something in that bag of yours that you can give me?"

"I'm afraid not," Cynthia said. "I have medicine for treating fever, salve for wounds, and tincture. But nothing for an upset stomach."

"And you call yourself a nurse?" The wagon swayed and Percy groaned. "Maybe I should walk. How about it, Mr. Prescott? Let me out and I'll gladly go on foot the rest of the way."

"Alone?" Prescott shook his head. "This is rugged country. There are grizzlies and mountain lions and hostiles. You're safer staying with us."

"Then maybe you would see fit to knock me out. Put me out of my misery until we reach the Silverlode."

Just then the wagon hit another hole, its front wheels bouncing like a child's ball. Percy was pitched against George Prescott, while Cynthia Howard was thrown across the narrow space that separated her from Fargo. He flung out his arms to catch her but she still slammed into him hard, her bosom flush against his chest, her face an inch from his, her raspberry lips almost brushing his mouth.

Blushing from neckline to hairline, Cynthia started to pull back but another lurch mashed her against Fargo yet again. Her mouth brushed his cheek, her breath warm on his neck. "Oh! Mercy me. I'm so sorry."

Fargo didn't mind one bit. He slid his hands under her arms to help her back to her seat, his thumbs rubbing against the bottoms of her sizeable breasts. "Glad you weren't hurt," he commented.

Cynthia smoothed her dress, flustered but trying not to show it. She accepted her bag and primly set it on her lap. "I'd forgotten how awful this road can be."

Artificial twilight shrouded them as the mud wagon clattered into the gorge. The temperature seemed to drop a few degrees. Thanks to the high rocky walls, the hammering of the team's hooves was amplified to thunderous proportions.

"This will only last a short while," Prescott said. He had to shout to be heard above the din.

Percy was doubled over, as green as lettuce. Biting into his leather carrying case, he gurgled like a two year old.

Fargo couldn't resist. "I sure could go for a nice, thick steak right about now. With a gallon of coffee to wash it down."

The accountant gurgled louder. Prescott gave Fargo a how-could-you? look, but Cynthia Howard covered her mouth with a hand to hide her grin.

One of the outriders gave a holler, and Fargo followed

the guard's pointed finger to the top of the gorge, and a thin object protruding over the edge. At first glance it appeared to be a rifle barrel. Fargo gripped the canvas roof and pulled himself to his feet, then swung out partway for a better look. Peering closer, he saw it was only a tree limb. No cause for alarm.

Fargo remained standing. He could see both walls, as well as the gorge mouth a few hundred yards ahead. The road was clear. No threats menaced them. But he still wasn't convinced Luther Keller had given up.

Abruptly, the driver hauled on the reins and bellowed for the team to halt. A huge boulder that had fallen from on high was now square in their path. Hopping down, the driver walked over to gauge whether the mud wagon would fit through the gap.

Cynthia leaned out to see what was going on. "Do you think that was done deliberately to slow us down?"

"No," Fargo said. Midway to the summit, he spotted a cavity where the boulder had been dislodged. No one could reach the spot from above or below. Wind, erosion, or some other natural factor was to blame.

The driver presently climbed back on the wagon. "Keep your arms and legs inside, folks," he called down. "It's going to be a mighty tight squeeze."

Fargo sat back down. The wagon creaked forward, angling between the boulder and the opposite wall. Exhibiting superb skill, the driver threaded it through with barely a whisker's width to spare on either side. Once in the clear, the team was held to a walk.

"We'll be stopping shortly," George Prescott announced.

"Why?" Fargo asked. A moving target was always harder to hit than a stationary one, and he said as much.

"I appreciate that," Prescott replied, "but we always stop on the far side of the gorge to rest the team for fifteen minutes or so."

A fact Keller was bound to know, Fargo realized. "Maybe you should make an exception just this once."

"Our driver, Lester, would throw a fit. He treats those horses as if they were his children. Pampers them silly, he does. Go ahead and suggest we stop, if you want, but it will fall upon deaf ears."

Fargo decided to not press the issue. The next leg of their route would tax the team to their utmost so it made sense to allow them a short breather. The dawn was quickly brightening. In a couple of minutes they rolled out into sunlight so brilliant, Fargo had to squint against the glare. He tensed, thinking that it would be another good spot for Keller's crowd to jump them, but no shots rang out.

Lester guided the wagon onto a gravel spur and brought it to a stop. "Stretch your legs, folks. But don't stray off. Last year a big old griz came wanderin' by this very spot and about scared the daylights out of us."

Hopping down, Fargo extended his arms to Cynthia. She accepted his help, leaning against him as he lowered her, her mouth curled in an enigmatic smile.

"I thank you, kind sir."

The riders had surrounded the wagon again. None of them dismounted, so it was up to the shotgun guard to take the water skin from the boot and give each of them a drink.

Percy Porter staggered onto the grass, sank onto his wobbly knees, and kissed the ground. "Thank you, God," he said. "Another five minutes and I'd have shot myself."

Fargo walked to the base of a slope speckled with shimmering aspens. At that altitude—six or seven thousand feet, well over a mile above sea level—the air had a cool tang, and he filled his lungs with its refreshing goodness.

"I always love it up this high," Cynthia remarked, joining him. "A little further on we'll be able to see clear back to Silver Flats."

"I take it you like your work."

"Who wouldn't? I help people. I tend the sick, treat wounds, relieve pain. I'd call that a worthwhile profession, wouldn't you?"

Fargo didn't have a chance to answer. She went on before he could.

"The only drawback is that I spend such long hours working day in and day out, that I have little time for myself. I can't remember the last time I was invited to a social or went on a buggy ride. Sometimes I feel so lonely, I could cry."

In that respect she reminded Fargo of Flora Flannigan.

"All my friends have long since married. Some are starting to tease me, saying if I'm not careful I'll wind up a spinster. Which is silly, but I can't help wondering. Is it just that I work too hard, or is it me?"

"You're a lovely woman," Fargo said. "Sooner or later the right man will come along and flatter that dress right off you."

Cynthia had a knack for blushing. "I'd say you're a bit of a flatterer, yourself." She paused. "What about you? Do you have a wife? A steady girl tucked away somewhere?"

"No to both," Fargo set her straight, "and no hankering to, either. I travel too much, blowing from place to place like a tumbleweed."

"I see." Cynthia fiddled with her black bag for a moment. "Still, I bet you find time for sparking and such. A handsome man like you must attract women like nectar attracts bees."

Fargo wondered if there was more to her statement than seemed apparent. "We all need to take time to smell the roses. As for any ladies I meet, if they show an interest in me, I generally don't make a habit of fighting them off with a club."

Cynthia laughed merrily. "That's nice to know. I wouldn't want to wind up with bruises and bumps all over me."

Fargo grinned. She had made it as plain as she could without giving him a formal invitation. Under different circumstances he would be all too willing to show her what she had been missing, but he had to control the urge until after they arrived at the mine. A man couldn't think straight when his manhood was as hard as iron, and he needed his wits about him now at all times.

One of the guards approached. Like the rest, he was a miner by trade, and had been pressed into service to help protect the payroll. Prescott had told Fargo that all six guards were crack shots, men who dropped deer and elk with but a single shot each and every time they went hunting.

Fargo hadn't said anything, but he didn't believe being a crack shot was enough, not in a life or death situation. A man also had to have the will to kill another person, the ability to look someone in the eyes and squeeze the trigger. Many couldn't do it. They just didn't have it in them. Not that they were cowards—they simply couldn't bring themselves to harm another human being, even if they were harmed themselves.

Fargo didn't think less of those who couldn't kill. He'd met quite a few, preachers and Mennonites and ordinary people who would rather be slain than slay. But he could never do as they did. He couldn't take a beating, or have hot lead flung at him, or cold steel brandished in his face, without doing to others exactly as they were doing to him.

When someone tried to hurt Fargo, he returned the favor. It was an instinct, as natural as breathing and sleeping. Some claimed it took a special talent to kill, and maybe they were right. But to his way of thinking, it was as much a sense of self-preservation as anything else.

The guard's words put an end to his idle musing. "We've found some tracks. Maybe you should have a look. I'm not much of a tracker but I can tell they're pretty fresh. I think they might spell trouble."

A sizeable body of riders, fifteen by Fargo's reckoning, had gone by about two hours ago. Evidently the tracks had been there on the road all along but Fargo had been in the mud wagon, unable to see underneath it, and none of the outriders had paid much attention to them.

Fargo gazed off down the road. The big question was

whether the tracks had been made by Keller's men. To find out, he went to George Prescott. "Did a bunch of miners head up to the Silverlode today on horseback?"

Prescott chuckled. "Miners aren't cowboys, my friend. They only ride when they absolutely must. Our crews go back and forth in wagons. Why?"

Fargo showed him the prints. "My guess is that the gunmen are up ahead, waiting for us. They could strike at any time." He nodded at the nurse and accountant. "Why not send Miss Howard and Porter back down? Lend them two of the guards' horses and have the guards ride in the wagon with us."

"I suppose it would be prudent," Prescott replied.

"Speaking for myself, I'm not going anywhere." Cynthia had strayed over and heard the conversation. "As many men as we have along, I feel perfectly safe."

"But if we're attacked, we'll be outnumbered," Fargo pointed out, "and our attackers will have the element of surprise."

"As well may be. But I refuse to go all the way back to town. I've come this far, and I'm determined to go the rest of the way." Cynthia walked off.

"A brave woman," Prescott remarked.

"A hardheaded woman," Fargo disagreed. They went over to the accountant, who had regained enough strength to stand. Some of the color was restored to his cheeks and he was breathing normally again.

Prescott told Porter about the tracks and what they might mean. "For your own safety, perhaps you should ride back to Silver Flats. You can check the company's books later this week," he told the accountant.

"And go through another horrible wagon ride?" Percy shook his head. "No, thank you. Besides, I'm not much of a horseman. I'd be so stiff and sore after the ride, I wouldn't be able to go anywhere for a month."

The driver, Lester, bellowed for them to load up.

Fargo didn't give up. He tried one more time as he

boosted Cynthia into the wagon. "You're making a mistake. The men who are after the payroll might not have any scruples about killing a woman."

Cynthia sat down, the bag in her lap. "I've made mistakes before. It's part of life. As for these elusive gunmen you're so worried about, I seriously doubt they will harm me. It's just not done."

Fargo didn't press her. It would be pointless. She had made up her mind, and, to a degree, she was right. To harm a woman on the frontier was unthinkable. Anyone who did was promptly hunted down and hanged. Even outlaws rarely violated the unwritten code of conduct that safeguarded the fairer sex like a shield. There were always exceptions, though, and something told Fargo that Luther Keller was one of them.

The wagon lurched forward. Percy, moaning, declared, "Oh, Lord! Here we go again. I wish God had given us wings so I could fly there."

Fargo levered a round into the Henry's chamber. It was only a matter of time now before all hell broke loose.

Only a matter of time.

7

Around the very next bend the road narrowed drastically, to where it was barely wider than the mud wagon. Ruts and holes were everywhere, severely jarring Skye Fargo and the other passengers. And there were sections where trees grew so close to the road's edge that sharp limbs thrust like sabers at the wagon's occupants, threatening to gouge out their eyes or rip off their ears if they leaned out too far.

The worst part of all, however, came a minute later when Percy glanced out his side and suddenly shrank back in terror. "Stop this thing or we'll all die!"

A sheer drop-off yawned below, a precipice hundreds of feet high. The wagon's wheels churned along the rim, less than a yard from the edge. A single misstep by the team or a misjudgment on Lester's part would hurtle them all into oblivion.

"Please!" Percy screeched, grabbing hold of George Prescott. "This is insane! Turn around before it's too late!"

"Calm yourself, Percival," George said. "There isn't room to turn around, even if that were an option. Which it isn't. We must see this through."

"I need a drink," Percy said, and slipped a silver flask from an inner pocket. Uncapping it, he gulped several times. But the liquor did little to restore his courage. He looked out again, whimpered, and clutched at his seat.

Cynthia Howard showed no fear whatsoever. She peered past the accountant into the depths of the abyss, and commented, "What a magnificent view. I do so love the mountains. They're spectacular."

"And dangerous," Fargo said.

The nurse smiled at him. "Is persistence your middle name? There's no more danger here than there is, say, in New York."

Fargo laughed.

"I'm serious. I've lived there, so I should know. Every week you hear about someone struck by a carriage. Every night thieves and robbers molest unsuspecting victims. In some parts of the city, it's not safe to be abroad after dark."

"New York doesn't have bears as big as buffalo. New York doesn't have mountain lions and rattlesnakes. Or hostile Indians who will lift your scalp after skinning you alive. Or badmen who will put a slug into you if you look at them crosswise."

Cynthia pursed her lovely lips. "I'm sorry, but there is nothing you can say that will convince me. I simply love these mountains."

So did Fargo, but he was practical enough to be wary of the perils that lurked just under their alluring surface. "Suit yourself."

The mud wagon rounded another bend and was finally clear of the cliff. Percy let out a long breath. "Thank God! I've never been so scared in my life."

Dense firs, shrouded in gloom, now hemmed them in. It was yet another ideal spot for an ambush, and Fargo was extra vigilant until they left the woodland in the dust. Then the wagon tilted as it began to climb the steepest grade yet. The driver's whip cracked and he hollered at the team, but the mud wagon soon slowed to a crawl.

"Anyone for a stroll?" George Prescott asked. "Usually at this point we get out and walk to the top to spare the horses."

"I would like that very much," Cynthia said.

"Sure." Percy was all too happy to oblige. "Anything to stop my insides from tossing around."

Prescott yelled for Lester to stop, which the grizzled driver promptly did. Again Fargo helped Cynthia down, and again she pressed her supple body against his in a manner that hinted she had more than a passing interest. The four of them fell into step behind the mud wagon, the rear guard only a dozen yards behind them.

They were high in the heart of the Rockies. Every side around them provided dazzling scenery. Majestic peaks towered to the clouds, those along the divide crowned white with caps of ivory snow. Elsewhere, stone ramparts reared like accusing fingers. Here and there stands of aspen rippled in the wind.

"See why I love it so?" Cynthia said.

The grade they were climbing became even steeper. Fargo was accustomed to hiking in the high mountains, but some of the others obviously weren't.

Percy, huffing and puffing as much from the altitude as from a lack of regular exercise, groused bitterly, "They have the gall to call this a road?"

"The surveyor we hired thought about having it swing to the south," Prescott mentioned, "but that would have made the trip eight miles longer than it already is."

"Surveyor?" Percy scoffed. "Did you check his credentials? Whoever picked this route was obviously missing a few marbles."

The top of the grade was just ahead. Fargo saw the three outriders disappear over the rim. Lester and the outrider with the shotgun were walking beside the team, Lester coaxing the horses on. Near the top he had to use his whip a few times. Then the wagon was up and over.

"Thank goodness," Percy said. "I wonder what difficulty awaits us next."

They found out the moment they cleared the crest. The three mounted guards had their hands in the air, and Lester and the shotgunner were frozen in place. Fargo instinctively started to level the Henry but a stern voice dissuaded him.

"I wouldn't, mister," Luther Keller's slippery voice said.

"Not unless you want us to gun down that beautiful creature next to you."

Keller wasn't alone. Fourteen gunmen formed a semicircle across the road, blocking further passage. Among them were faces familiar to Fargo. They included Harvey, Keller's shadow, and Billy Pardee. Decker was there, and the Texan with the icy eyes, as well as Po and Calhoun, the scarecrow.

Pardee nodded. "How-do, big man. I've been lookin' forward to runnin' into you again. I figure to take you down a notch or three."

"Enough posturing, Billy," Keller snapped. "I'll do the talking. Your job is to keep quiet and shoot anyone I tell you to."

The rear guards were just now coming over the rim. One of them tried to bring his rifle to bear but stopped when half a dozen muzzles were swung in his direction.

"Wise decision," Keller said.

Prescott, Fargo noticed, was stunned, standing there with his mouth agape.

"What's the matter, George?" Keller asked him. "Cat got your tongue? Are all the pieces of the puzzle beginning to fall into place? Are you kicking yourself for not realizing the truth sooner?"

"Luther? It was *you*? You've been behind everything?" Prescott lifted his right hand and touched his face as if to assure himself he wasn't dreaming. "How can this be? The Anaheim Consortium picked you to be my assistant. They put you in a position of trust, of great responsibility, and this is how you repay them? Why, man? In God's name, *why*?"

Luther Keller dismounted and handed the reins of his mount to Harvey. Clasping his hands behind his back, he casually strolled past the three lead guards and the mud wagon. "I can't tell you how much I've looked forward to this day, George. The expression on your face alone has made it all worthwhile."

"I don't understand, Luther," Prescott said in a bewildered tone. "I honestly don't."

"Of course not. You never have been very perceptive, George," Keller responded. "Let's be frank, shall we? You have the intelligence of a cow. Yet our illustrious employers saw fit to select you over me."

"They did what?"

"You didn't know? We were both in the running to manage the Silverlode. We've both had identical experience, and our work records were spotless. Yet they picked you, then threw me the bone of being your assistant."

Prescott snapped his fingers. "So that's what this is about? You've been harboring a grudge all this time and this is your way of getting back at them, and at me."

"Your brain must be the size of a pea," Keller said in disgust. "Don't flatter yourself. Yes, I was mad. But it was just the latest in along string of disappointments. Twice before I was up for lucrative appointments and each time they chose someone else."

"And you took it personally?" Prescott said. "Luther, I was passed over several times before they finally gave me a position in management. It's fairly routine. If you were so upset, why didn't you talk it out with them? Surely any alternative is better than stealing company payrolls and causing production delays, possibly jeopardizing the entire future of the mine."

Keller looked at Fargo. "Do you believe how stupid he is? The man is in charge of one of the richest mines in the country, yet he can't add two plus two. You did, though, Fargo. You suspected from the very beginning."

Prescott turned. "Is he right, Mr. Fargo? Did you know he was involved all along? If so, why wasn't I informed?"

"You wouldn't have believed me," Fargo said. "Not without proof. And Keller was too clever at covering his tracks. He had Flynn Flannigan killed when Flannigan began to suspect him of being up to no good. He had Irish Mike murdered because he had heard me say I'd bumped into some gunmen who were looking for him. And you know about the two attempts on my life."

Horror lined Prescott's features. "If not for revenge, then why, Luther? Why?"

Keller was still staring at Fargo. "You must have some idea. Tell this idiot."

"I knew there had to be more at stake than the payrolls," Fargo said. "It had to be something worth a lot more for Keller to go to all the trouble of importing gunmen and risk prison or a noose by having people killed."

"But what else could it be?" Prescott was at a loss.

"The mine," Fargo said. "He wants the mine for himself."

"The Silverlode? But that's ridiculous. The Anaheim Consortium owns it."

"Keller doesn't want to own it. He wants to run it. To be put in charge so he can do as he pleases. So he can steal silver without anyone being the wiser. A little here, a little there, and in a few years he'll be a rich man."

"A *very* rich man," Keller said. "All it will take are a few miners in my back pocket, as it were. I calculate I can siphon off a quarter of a million dollars' worth without arousing suspicion. Enough to live on comfortably for the rest of my natural life."

Percy Porter spoke up. "It will never work, sir. The consortium insists on accurate records. Siphoning ore would be detected."

"Not if the books are doctored," Keller said.

"Doctor the *ledgers*?" Percy was aghast, making it sound as if it were a greater crime than murder. "Why, that's positively heinous! I must protest in the strongest possible terms."

Keller snorted. "Protest all you want, scribbler. In a little while what you think won't matter."

George Prescott was still absorbing the full impact of his assistant's treachery. "So you sabotaged the mine to make me look bad in the consortium's eyes, and did all the rest just so you can take over in my stead?"

"Now you're catching on." Keller beamed. "I'm the logical choice to be your replacement. Especially after the secret reports I've been submitting."

"Secret reports?"

"On how inept you are. How your incompetence led to the problems we've been having. How your blunders cost needless work delays." Keller was pleased with himself and it showed. "Why, I even told them how you ignored warnings about an outlaw gang in the area and failed to add extra guards to the last payroll run. So I took the stage myself, to keep watch."

"And helped yourself to the strongbox," Fargo said.

"Three of my men did. They were hiding near the relay station. When the driver and the shotgun guard went inside, I signaled them."

"My God!" Prescott declared, placing a hand on his brow.

"Is the truth finally sinking in?" Keller mocked him. "My scheme is brilliant, if I do say so myself. I've played you like a fish on the end of a line. No one will shed a tear when your body turns up. The Anaheim Consortium will blame your own negligence in not having enough guards along. Within a month I'll be officially appointed as your successor. I'll have total control of the Silverlode."

"What about us?" Percy asked.

"What about you? Didn't you hear Mr. Fargo? I don't believe in leaving witnesses around."

The accountant pointed at Cynthia. "Don't tell me you'd kill a woman?"

"For a quarter of a million dollars I would kill my own mother." Luther Keller's greed oozed from every pore. "I'm sorry, Miss Howard. But you can see how it is."

"All I see," Cynthia said, "is a vile monster, a loathsome slug who should be stepped on and crushed."

Keller wasn't the least bit angry. "My, my. Such a mouth

on such an attractive lady. If I were truly the abomination you claim, I'd turn you over to my men. Instead, I'll grant you the same swift end I'm granting the others."

"For that I should be grateful?" Cynthia said scornfully.

George Prescott took a half step forward. "Please, Luther. I beg you. Do what you will with me but spare everyone else. They're not to blame for the injustices you think you've suffered."

Keller sighed. "You still don't understand, do you? I just want the money, George. Lots and lots of money. I want to be filthy, stinking rich. I can't make it any plainer."

Prescott scowled. "You're despicable, Luther. Truly and utterly rotten to the core. How can you value money more than—"

The question was never finished. Keller brought his right fist up in a tight arc, his knuckles connecting with the point of Prescott's chin, rocking him back. Prescott stumbled against Percy Porter, who grabbed hold of him to keep from being knocked over.

"Who are you to judge me?" Keller hissed. "Maybe you're willing to slave your life away for a pittance, but I'm not. I want to enjoy myself while I still can. I want to travel, be with beautiful women. London, Paris, Greece— I'll visit them all before I'm through."

Fargo had listened enough. "Have your men drop their guns. We're taking you down to Silver Flats and handing you over to Marshal Withers."

Keller faced him. "Did my ears deceive me? You're dictating terms? And here I credited you with more intellect than George. Apparently I was wrong." He motioned at the gun sharks. "All I need do is say the word and they'll cut you down where you stand."

"Will they?" Fargo said. "Do you want to take that chance when you're between them and me?"

The blunder Keller had made in coming over to boast began to register. "I wouldn't advise trying anything. I've hired only the best. Most of them can shoot the center out of a playing card at twenty paces."

"Playing cards don't move," Fargo said, "and they don't shoot back." He wagged the Henry. "Your second mistake was in not making us drop our hardware." The lead outriders still had their pistols, while the guards at the rear had both their rifles and their revolvers trained on the gun sharks. "Give the order to shoot and you'll be one of the first to die."

Luther Keller licked his thin lips. He looked to the right and the left. Overconfidence had made him careless and he did not like it one bit. "So will the nurse." He grasped at a straw. "Do you want her life on your conscience?"

Prescott answered. "Strange words coming from a man who doesn't have one."

"You aim to riddle us with slugs anyway," Fargo said. "We might as well go down fighting." To demonstrate, he sprang, letting go of the Henry and wrapping his left arm around Keller's throat, whipping out his Colt all in one swift, smooth movement. The Colt was now cocked, the barrel gouging into Keller's temple before any of the gunmen could react. "If your men try anything, you die."

Keller struggled a moment until he felt the hard muzzle digging into his skin. Some of the gunmen extended their weapons, ready to fire, but Keller frantically waved them off. "No! No! He'll kill me!"

Harvey's mouth twitched in suppressed fury. "This won't help you none," he snarled at Fargo. "You're only delaying it."

"Drop your guns or he dies!" Fargo shouted.

"Like Hell!" Harvey was no fool. "You won't shoot Luther. Because if you do, we'll cut all of you to pieces."

It was a stalemate. But all it would take to unleash a hailstorm of hot lead was a single wrong move. Fargo didn't like how several of the guards behind him were tensing up as if preparing to resort to their firearms. "Don't anyone do anything!" he cautioned.

Harvey was whispering to the gunhands. At a nod from him, they wheeled their animals and trotted into the trees. To Fargo's relief, the company's guards held their fire.

Billy Pardee was the last to ride off, but not without a parting comment. "You reckon you've won, don't you, big man? But you're wrong, dead wrong. We're about to teach you a lesson, Texas-style."

"Stop them!" Percy cried, fumbling in his jacket for his derringer. He brought it out but by then the hired killers were gone, melting into the vegetation like a pack of wolves slinking off to lick their wounds.

George Prescott clapped Fargo on the shoulder. "Your quick thinking saved us! They won't dare try to harm us so long as we have Luther."

"You're wrong if you think they're licked," Fargo said.

In confirmation, a blistering firestorm thundered from the firs. "Get down!" Fargo yelled. Dropping, he pulled Keller down with him. But the shots weren't directed at him or any of the others. The heavy slugs smashed into the team and into the horses belonging to the guards. Again and again Fargo heard the sickening smack of lead striking horseflesh as the terrified animals squealed and whinnied in torment. Bedlam erupted, with the guards trying to get their mounts out of the range of fire. The three nearest the rim had the best chance, but their horses were shot out from under them before they had gone two yards.

It was over within seconds. The six horses that made up the team and every last mount was down, riddled with holes and oozing blood, either thrashing and nickering or lying as still as tombstones. One of the guards had been creased in the arm, another had been shot in the leg. But no one had been killed—yet.

Grating laughter pealed from the forest. "Like I told you, big man, you haven't won yet! Not by a long shot."

Some of the guards fired into the woods, wildly working their rifles. They were wasting ammunition. Fargo shouted for them to stop, and when the shots tapered off, he roughly hauled Luther Keller erect.

The mastermind was smiling. He smoothed his jacket, adjusted his bowler, and said, "Why not make it easy on yourselves? Let me go. You'll never live long enough to turn me over to the law."

"We like your company too much," Fargo said, and drove the Henry into Keller's groin. As Keller folded, grunting and gurgling, Fargo cupped a hand to his mouth. "Pardee! Billy Pardee!"

There were several seconds of silence, then, "I hear you, big man. You shouldn't ought to have done that!"

"I'll do it again, or worse, if one more shot is fired at us. Just one. You hear me?"

"I hear you." Pardee sounded as if he were seething mad. "But you hear me, you buckskin bastard. I'm makin' it my personal business to put you under snakes. You ain't got long to live, so make the most of what's left."

Everyone else was back on their feet. George Prescott was examining a tear in his sleeve. "He's bluffing. They won't lift a finger against us so long as we have their boss."

A sob drew Fargo's attention to the team. Lester was on his knees, his arms flung over one of the horses.

"What do we do now?" Percy Porter asked. "Sit here and wait for help to come?"

Cynthia had smudges all over her formerly spotless white dress. "Surely they'll start to miss us at the mine when the mud wagon doesn't arrive on time. They'll send out a search party, won't they?"

"Eventually," Prescott said. "They'll be expecting us about three. When we don't show up by four, they'll think we must have left Silver Flats later than usual. By five they'll start to debate what to do. By six they'll decide to send some men. But they won't find us by dark and might decide to make camp until morning, then resume the search."

"So you're saying we're on our own until tomorrow morning?" Percy said.

"That would be my guess, yes. The man in charge of the Silverlode when Luther and I are gone, Vern Rowley, isn't the most decisive of individuals. He's dependable, but he won't so much as sneeze without being told."

Keller was struggling to stand, his face scarlet. Venom sizzled in his eyes, directed at Fargo. "Vern Rowley is a jackass. He'll hem and haw and won't decide to send out a search party until tomorrow morning at the earliest. By then all of you will be dead."

Percy pointed his derringer at Keller. "You're forgetting something, aren't you?"

"Capturing me won't stop my men, you little weasel. I've promised each of them more money than they've ever seen at any one time in their whole lives. They're not about to let anything happen to me."

Fargo had been mulling over what to do. "I wonder," he said thoughtfully, and moved to the back of the mud wagon, pulling Keller with him. The others drifted along.

"What are you up to?" Prescott inquired as Fargo untied the flap to gain access to the boot.

"The payroll total comes to fifteen thousand dollars, correct?"

"Slightly more than that, yes."

"And there are fourteen gunmen," Fargo said, flipping the flap aside. There sat the strongbox, tied in place with rope.

"So?"

Fargo turned around. "So we give them the money. We pay each of them a thousand dollars to ride off and leave us in peace."

Prescott blinked. "You can't be serious."

"Why not? That's how much Keller promised them. Once they have their money, they'll go. Then we'll camp here until the search party shows." Fargo liked his plan— they would all live to see another day, and Luther Keller would get his due, either behind bars or, more than likely, dangling from a rope.

"Do you honestly expect me to turn the strongbox over to a pack of miserable vermin?" George Prescott said.

"If it will save lives, why not? It's only money."

"Money desperately needed by the miners and their families. No, I forbid it. The Silverlode Mine doesn't pander to common criminals. We'll start for the mine immediately and take the strongbox with us."

"Lug that heavy thing all the way to the mine?" Fargo said. It had to weigh over a hundred pounds. Normally, that wasn't so much. But they would be constantly climbing steep slopes, in rarified air, making it twice as hard.

"We'll have the men take turns, two at a time," Prescott said. "It shouldn't pose much of a problem." He raised a hand when Fargo went to speak. "I won't hear another word about turning the payroll over to those scum. You're working for me, in case you've forgotten, and you'll do as I damn well say." He stalked off toward the guards.

Fargo clenched his fists. The fool was dooming them all.

"See what I've had to put up with?" Luther Keller said, smirking. "Mark my words, mister. Before this is done, you'll wish to hell you'd shot him yourself."

8

They started out half an hour later. Two of the guards walked ahead, two more trailed a dozen yards to the rear. Skye Fargo tried to convince George Prescott to change his mind but the man stubbornly refused. "We'll all make it," the manager insisted, "with the payroll intact. I'll prove to the Anaheim Consortium that their trust in me wasn't misplaced. I'll expose all the lies in the secret reports Luther has sent."

The cause of their ordeal was enjoying himself immensely. Keller turned to grin at Fargo frequently. They both knew Prescott was making a grave mistake that would benefit Keller. But there was nothing Fargo could do, short of knocking George Prescott out and forcing everyone else to do as he wanted at gunpoint. Some of the guards were bound to buck him, forcing Fargo to spill innocent blood.

Resigned to seeing the lunacy through, Fargo hiked up the road with the rest. Keller was in front, where he could keep an eye on him. On Fargo's left was Cynthia Howard, behind him were the accountant and Prescott.

An unnaturally still forest hemmed the road. It should be alive with the chirping of birds and the noisy antics of squirrels and chipmunks, but it was eerily quiet. Fargo knew the gunmen were in there somewhere, shadowing them. Sooner or later Billy Pardee would make his move, and thanks to Prescott's bullheadedness, the gunmen would pick them off like clay targets at a shooting match.

"Why so glum?" Cynthia asked.

"Should I be happy about getting a bullet in the back?" Fargo responded

"Are you one of those people who always expect the worst?" She clucked like a mother hen. "Really, a grown man like you should know better. My philosophy is to always look at the bright side of things."

"Even when there is none?"

"I'd never have taken you for a worrywart. We're alive, aren't we? Keller's men don't dare jump us, not when we have him. I'd say we have things well in hand."

"Me, too." Percy had been listening. "If those cutthroats try anything, I'll empty my derringer into their leader."

"All two shots?" Fargo said.

George Prescott had to add his opinion. "You mystify me. I was led to believe frontiersmen are bold and adventurous. Yet you're acting quite the opposite. How have you survived in the wilds as long as you have when you worry so much over trifles? It's almost comical."

Fargo didn't consider being bushwhacked a trifle, but all he said was, "You can poke fun at me all you want if we reach the Silverlode."

"*When* we reach it, you mean." Prescott brimmed with the conviction they would. "I'll expect an apology from you for giving me such a hard time. I'm not the incompetent Luther would have everyone believe."

Fargo was beginning to have his doubts. How was it Prescott never thought to post guards at the mine to keep the equipment from being sabotaged? Why didn't he realize that whoever was to blame had to be someone in authority, someone who knew the workings of the mine inside-out and could strike with impunity? And why in the world hadn't Prescott thought more about the fact that Keller was on the very stage the first payroll was snatched from?

They climbed for over two hours, the road winding steadily upward, the guards taking turns toting the heavy strongbox. Upon reaching a grassy shelf, Prescott called a halt so everyone could rest.

Ahead was another steep slope strewn with large boulders. Fargo scanned it but saw no movement. He was surprised the gunmen hadn't done anything yet. The longer Pardee waited, the better the chance of a search party arriving and putting an end to any likelihood of freeing Luther Keller.

The trek was taking its toll. Everyone was sweating and tired. Fargo removed his hat and mopped his forehead with his bandanna, then retied it around his neck.

Seated a few feet away, Keller wore his smirk like a second suit. "It won't be long now. I feel it in my bones."

Fargo tapped the Henry. "That won't be all you feel."

"Don't kid yourself," Keller said. "Pardee's shrewd. You'll be the first one he puts a slug into." Keller leaned back. "There's one thing I'd like to know before that happens, though. Why did you butt in? All you had to do was ride on out of Silver Flats without saying a word to anyone and you'd be long gone by now. You'd be safe."

"You convinced me to stay."

"Me?" Keller sat back up. "Like hell I did! I tried to have you killed. Not once, but twice. I didn't want you to tell anyone else that you had run into three gunmen who were looking for me."

"That's what did it." Out of the corner of an eye, Fargo thought he glimpsed something on the slope above. But when he looked, he saw only boulders and a few clumps of dry weeds waving in the breeze.

"You're not making any sense," Keller said.

"I take it personal when someone tries to kill me. If you hadn't tried to have me gunned down, I'd have left the next morning."

"So you're saying your involvement is my fault?"

"More or less."

Keller shrugged. "If I had it to do all over again, I'd do it the same. I don't believe in leaving loose ends lying around—and you were certainly a loose end." He nodded at the others. "Now all of them are, too. Once I've disposed of them, the Silverlode is mine."

Fargo plucked a blade of grass and stuck it between his teeth. "You're putting the cart before the horse."

"Am I? We'll see." Keller squinted up at the sun. "Very soon, too, I should think. Twenty-four hours from now I'll be sipping whiskey in celebration and buzzards will be feasting on your carcass."

"As you say, we'll see," Fargo retorted. But he wasn't as confident as he pretended to be. In fact, a growing feeling of unease brought him to his feet.

No one else betrayed the least bit of alarm. Several of the guards were keeping watch, others were taking it easy. Prescott and Percy were involved in a discussion of cost overruns at the mine, while the driver and the shotgun guard were debating the merits of a fallen dove they both knew.

Fargo tried to will himself to relax but he couldn't. Cynthia was helping herself to a sip of water from the water skin and he walked over to do the same. "How are you holding up?" he asked.

"Just fine. If not for Keller's killers, I'd be enjoying myself greatly. I love the outdoors. And I love long walks." Cynthia tilted the skin to her mouth and swallowed. When she lowered it, beads of water dotted her luscious lower lip. "I rarely get to indulge my passion for either."

Her comment spurred Fargo into speculating on whether she indulged in any other sort of passion. The way she had rubbed against him, the enticing sway of her slender hips when she walked, hinted that under her prim exterior smoldered desires and yearnings, the kind of which Fargo was aching to let loose.

"Care for some?" Cynthia questioned, extending the water skin.

"Don't mind if I do." Fargo leaned the Henry against his left leg and reached out. As he did, the rifle shifted and fell.

Automatically, he bent to grab it, not realizing that doing so would save his life. For at the selfsame instant he bent down, a rifle cracked and a slug meant to core his skull thudded into the ground behind him.

Other shots thundered out. Three of the payroll guards were slain in the first volley. The rest dived flat and returned fire. There was no cover on the grassy shelf. They were all easy targets.

Fargo snapped up the Henry, sighted on a figure that popped out from behind a boulder, and fired, having the satisfaction of seeing the gunman stagger and drop. He saw the shotgun guard take a slug in the shoulder and Lester winged in the leg. The gun sharks were cutting them to ribbons. Unless they got off that shelf, they would all be dead in a matter of minutes. "Back down the road!" Fargo yelled, pumping his arm. "We can't stay here!"

No one heard. The boom of rifles and the crack of pistols, the gritty curses and shrill screams, all drowned out his shout. Another hardcase appeared, taking a bead on the driver, Lester. Lester didn't spot him but Fargo did, and a .44 slug to the brain spared Lester from further harm.

"We have to get out of here!" Fargo repeated. Grabbing Cynthia's wrist, he backpedaled. On his left, another guard from the mine fell. Up on the slope he counted at least five bodies. The rest of the gunmen were blazing away, firing as fast as they could.

The only reason Prescott's party hadn't already been slaughtered was that few of the hardcases had repeaters. Most were single-shot Sharps or other models, which took time to reload.

Of all those involved, only Fargo had a Henry. The finest, most expensive rifle manufactured, it held sixteen rounds in a tubular magazine under the barrel. If any of Prescott's group were to make it off the shelf alive, it was up to Fargo to pin the killers down long enough for those who could to escape.

Accordingly, on reaching the edge, Fargo gave Cynthia a

shove that sent her stumbling. Then he spun and brought the Henry to bear. Calhoun was visible. The scarecrow was taking careful aim at someone else. He never realized Fargo had him in his own sights, and at the crash of the Henry, Calhoun's days of murder for hire came to an end.

The firing momentarily tapered. Fargo took advantage to try once more. "Prescott! Percy! The rest of you! Get out of here! Go back the way we came!" This time they finally heard him.

Only two of the guards were still standing. They quickly retreated, firing as they did. Lester was down, sprawled in a spreading pool of scarlet. The shotgun guard had half his face missing. Another man was trying to crawl to safety but he had been shot to pieces and was bleeding like a sieve. After a few feet he cried out, and died.

Too late, Fargo remembered Luther Keller. The mastermind was nowhere to be seen. Raising the Henry, Fargo began firing repeatedly, methodically, at any gunman who showed himself, making them hunt cover long enough for everyone else to dash past him. Just as George Prescott ran by, Billy Pardee materialized and snapped off a shot. Fargo swiveled but the young Texan ducked behind a boulder.

Banging off several more rounds, Fargo spun and flew down the road on the heels of the others. Prescott was stooped over, a hand clasped to his side. Percy still held his carrying case pressed to his chest, as if to ward off bullets. They were all fleeing in a panic except for Cynthia, who had stopped and was looking back.

Fargo had to get them off the road. As soon as the gunmen regrouped, they would mount up and give chase. "Into the trees!" he hollered, pointing at the pines that fringed the south edge. "Into the trees!"

The accountant and the two guards immediately obeyed but George Prescott had slowed and was shuffling painfully along. Cynthia rushed to help him.

Fargo caught up with them just as Cynthia slipped an

arm around Prescott's waist. He added one of his own. "How bad is it?"

Prescott glanced up. Through clenched teeth he said, "I can manage. Don't worry about me."

A carpet of pine needles cushioned their footfalls. Percy and the guards had only gone about twenty yards and stopped to wait for them in a small clearing. Fargo and Cynthia lowered Prescott, and while she knelt to examine him, Fargo turned to the two miners. Both wore homespun clothes and black boots. "What are your names?"

"Burns, sir," responded one who sported a wooly mustache on his upper lip.

"I'm Titus." A red furrow on his left cheek showed how close Titus had come to not making it through the last barrage of lead thrown at them by Keller's men.

"I want all of us to get out of this alive, so from here on out you do exactly as I say. Our only hope is to reach the Silverlode Mine."

George Prescott tilted his head. "Now hold on," he said, and coughed. "Those men still work for me and they'll follow my orders, not yours. I want them to sneak on back and retrieve the strongbox."

Burns and Titus looked at one another.

"It will get them killed," Fargo said.

"Not if they're careful," Prescott argued. "They can hide and wait until the bandits aren't looking, then grab it."

Fargo could tell the two miners would rather wrestle an enraged wolverine. "How far do you think they would get lugging that heavy box?"

Prescott tried to sit up and winced. "I refuse to let Keller have it! We can't let him win! No matter the cost."

"Titus and Burns stay with us," Fargo said flatly. "Their lives are more important than the payroll."

"How dare you!" Incensed, Prescott attempted to stand but he only managed to get to one knee before sinking back down with a groan.

Cynthia gripped his arm. She had slipped his jacket off

and unbuttoned his shirt. "Don't try that again! You'll make yourself worse. Sit still so I can tend you."

"You don't understand," Prescott said weakly. "None of you do. Luther Keller has tried everything in his power to ruin me. I can't let him succeed. I'm responsible for getting that money safely to the mine."

"You're also responsible for the men you picked to guard it," Fargo said. "Or don't you care that six of them died protecting your precious strongbox?"

Prescott grew angrier. "Of course I care! That's not the issue! The point is that—" Stiffening, he inhaled loudly, then started to tip over.

"Enough!" Cynthia slowly lowered him to the ground. "Keep quiet, please, until I'm done." She parted his shirt and probed front and back with skilled fingers. When she was done, she rose and stepped closer to Fargo.

"Well?"

"He took a bullet just below his right shoulder blade. It went clean through and came out below his rib cage. There's a lot of internal damage, but exactly how much or whether he'll live, I just can't say."

"Can he walk if he has to?" Fargo asked. They couldn't stay where they were much longer. The hired gunmen would be after them any minute.

"Moving him will only make him worse. He's bleeding inside. I'm not a surgeon or I'd cut him open here and now." Cynthia looked down at the blood on her hands. "I could still try, though."

Fargo weighed Prescott's life in the balance against those of the others. If they took the time to try and save him, all six of them would assuredly die. If they moved on, maybe only Prescott would. Five lives against Prescott's one. "Bandage him as best you can. We're heading out."

Cynthia hesitated.

"If we don't leave, now, Keller will catch us. Is that what you want?"

Reluctantly, Cynthia bent over Prescott, taking a bandage roll from her black bag. "Give me another minute."

Fargo turned to the accountant, who had sat down and was clasping his knees to his chest and rocking back and forth in utter misery. "This can't be happening," Percy mewed over and over. "It just can't."

Fargo hunkered in front of him. "It is. And if you want to live through it, you need to control your fear."

Percy extended his right hand. In it was his prized derringer. "I couldn't shoot. I tried. I aimed at one of them but I couldn't bring myself to pull the trigger."

"Some people can't," Fargo said.

"But they were trying to kill us!" Percy practically screamed. "What kind of man am I? I can't even defend myself!" Tears streaked his cheeks and he shook the derringer as if he were strangling it. "I'm just a coward, is what I am! A rotten coward!"

To be kind and considerate and take the time to calm Percy down were luxuries denied Fargo. Instead, he hauled off and slapped him, nearly knocking the accountant over. Then he gripped him by the shoulders. "A lot of men freeze up the first time. It doesn't make you yellow. Forget about it for now. We need to work together now, or none of us will survive."

Percy's lower lip trembled and for a second Fargo thought he would start bawling like an infant, but he had more grit than he credited himself with. Sniffling, Percy nodded. "Very well. I'll do my part. And the next time I'm put to the test, I won't let you down."

"That's the spirit." Fargo clapped him on the arm and rose.

Burns and Titus were anxiously awaiting instructions. "What about us?" the latter inquired. "What do you want us to do?"

"Follow behind us," Fargo said. "If you spot Keller's outfit, come running. Don't tangle with them by yourselves."

Burns snorted. "Don't worry on that score, mister. I have a wife and a slew of young'uns, and I aim to see them all again sometime soon."

Cynthia had finished bandaging George Prescott, who had passed out from pain. Fargo slid his arm under Prescott's right shoulder, and motioned for Percy to take the other side. Together, they hoisted the manager erect. Moving as quickly as the terrain allowed, the six of them hurried to the southwest. At Fargo's request Cynthia carried the Henry. Titus and Burns trailed behind some twenty to thirty yards, but always kept in sight. Periodically Prescott would groan and his eyelids would flutter, but he didn't revive.

"Every step puts him closer to the grave," Cynthia remarked.

"It can't be helped," Fargo said. As with so many things in life, circumstances often dictated what a person had to do. Not what they *wanted* to do, what they *had* to do— whether they liked it or not.

"We could hide him somewhere. I could stay and nurse him while you and the rest lead Keller away."

"And leave you alone?" Fargo opposed the idea for several reasons, not the least of which was the outcome should Keller find her. Keller's previous comment notwithstanding, Fargo wouldn't put it past him to turn her over to Pardee and company to do with as they pleased.

"I'm a grown woman. I can take care of myself."

Fargo was sure she could—except if she was pitted against these ornery badmen. "It's best if we stick together," he tactfully replied.

Over thirty minutes of tough travel brought them to a wide ravine that angled up the mountain. Fargo entered it, noting how steep it was and the scant cover between the bottom and a pine-covered bench at the top. As they scaled the rim, Percy tottered and nearly lost hold of Prescott.

"I'm sorry. I can't go another step. I'm exhausted."

All three of them were winded. "We'll rest here a spell,"

Fargo announced. They lowered Prescott onto a patch of grass, then Fargo claimed the Henry and stared down into the ravine, mentally debating whether the idea he had was worth attempting.

Titus and Burns caught up, Burns wheezing noisily from the climb. "My lungs ain't what they should be," he divulged. "Working in mines all my life is to blame. So much dust and stuff, a man can't hardly breathe at times. It takes a toll."

"Then why be a miner?" Percy was curious.

"It's all I know. It's all I've ever been." Burns gave himself a whack on the chest and his wheezing lessened. "Sometimes a fella gets stuck in a rut and can't get out." Leaning on his rifle, he asked, "How long can we rest?"

Fargo pivoted on the heel of his left boot. "As long as you need. We're not going anywhere for a while."

Cynthia, checking Prescott's bandage, looked up. "Why? What do you have in mind?"

"Ending it right down there." Fargo indicated the pines that grew along the lip of the bench. "What worked for them can work for us. We'll lie in wait and ambush Keller's gunnies as they come up. There's not much cover for them to use. If we do it right, maybe we can kill enough to make the rest see fit to give up."

The accountant and the two miners walked to the edge. Percy gazed down, his face scrunched in doubt. "Are you sure it will work? There are more of them than there are of us."

"And they'll be on their guard," Titus said. "At the first shot they'll cut loose with all they have."

"Let them," Fargo said. "We'll have the advantage of higher ground, and we'll be behind trees. They'll be right out in the open."

"These are quick-trigger artists we're talking about," Burns said. "Men who make their living by shooting folks. They practice day in and day out. Don't try to pull the wool over our eyes by claiming none of us will take a slug."

"There's no predicting what will happen," Fargo admitted, "but we'll certainly have the edge."

"How many do you figure we'd have to drop for the rest to leave us be?" Titus asked. "Five? Six?"

"Just one."

The three men looked at Fargo as if he were addlepated. "Making wolf meat out of only one of them won't make a difference," Percy said.

"It will if the one we shoot is Luther Keller."

Percy grinned in vengeful glee. "I get it. Kill their leader and the gunmen will have no reason to kill us."

"But it's not as if Keller will ride up to us with open arms," Titus said.

"I can't promise you it will work," Fargo stressed, growing tired of their quibbling. "I'll leave it up to you since our lives are at stake. Either we make a stand or we keep on running. Which will it be? We'll put it to a vote."

"I vote we ambush the sons of bitches," Percy said.

Burns removed his floppy hat and ran a hand through his black hair. "I'm sorry. I vote we don't."

Everyone stared at Titus. He studied the ravine, glanced at Burns, then studied the ravine again. "It might work. It just might. And if we can end it now, we'll save ourselves a heap of trouble."

"And possibly save George Prescott's life," Cynthia observed. "The less we move him, the better off the poor man will be. So I say we should stand up to Luther and his paid guns, come what may."

"That makes it four in favor, one against." Fargo tallied the count. "But I won't make you lend a hand, Burns, if you don't want to."

"I'll do my part," the miner said. "I just have an awful feeling about this, is all. I don't know how to describe it, but it gives me the shivers."

Titus gave his friend a playful nudge. "You always have been a fretter by nature. Remember that time you refused to go into shaft number twelve because you were sure it was going to collapse? It never did. And the time you swore to high heaven a ghost was roaming the lower tunnels but it turned out to be a stray cat? And the—"

Burns held up a hand. "Enough. I said I'd help out, didn't I? What more do you want?"

"A keg of black powder to roll down on Keller would be nice," Fargo joked, and they laughed. Only he was in earnest. Having the high ground in and of itself wasn't enough. Not against seasoned killers like Pardee and Decker. The two miners and the accountant had put their trust in him, and he could only hope, with every fiber of his being, that his brainstorm wouldn't turn out to be the death of them.

9

It was said Apache warriors could squat on their haunches for hours on end and it wouldn't bother them in the least. Skye Fargo was no Apache, but he had been squatting behind a pine for almost an hour and had not moved once except for an occasional turn of his head.

The same couldn't be said of the two miners and Percy Porter. The three constantly shifted, scratched, grunted, and sniffed. Not one of them could sit still for more than two minutes. Fortunately, thanks to the steepness of the ravine, the gunmen wouldn't be able to see into the trees until they were almost on top of them.

Fargo wasn't worried that his companions would spoil the ambush. He was beginning to wonder, however, if the gun sharks would ever show up. He'd expected them long ago. Their absence did not bode well, although exactly why they had been delayed eluded him.

Resigned to a longer wait, Fargo glanced to his left at Titus, who was chewing on a twig, then to his right at the others. Burns was having trouble staying awake. His chin kept bobbing, and he kept jerking his head up. Percy had collected a handful of small pebbles and was dropping them, one by one, into a small circle he had drawn in the dirt. When he was done, he picked up the pebbles and started all over again.

Their lives were at stake, Fargo mused, and the accountant was playing a game. He wasn't surprised. What had surprised him, though, was when Percy demanded to play a part even though the only gun he had was the derringer. Its range was ten feet in the hands of a competent marksman, which Percy definitely wasn't. The gunmen would have to be within spitting distance for Percy to be able to hit one.

Over a boulder, George Prescott was resting, asleep. Cynthia sat by his side, her forearms on her knees. She caught Fargo's eye and smiled warmly. Her hair was slightly disheveled and her dress was a mess but she was as lovely as ever, her red lips like candies just waiting to be sucked on.

Fargo tore his gaze from her and concentrated on the task at hand. There was a proper time and a place for everything. Fargo turned to stare down into the ravine, and tensed at what he saw.

A lone rider had appeared in the shade of a spruce, a gunman in a brown vest and hat. He held a rifle, and he was scanning the ravine from bottom to top.

"They're here," Fargo whispered.

Percy dropped the pebbles and drew his derringer. Titus and Burns lifted their rifles to their shoulders.

"Remember, don't fire until I say so," Fargo reminded them. "We want them close, so damn close that we can't possibly miss."

The rider nudged his mount into the open. Dismounting, he examined the ground, then rose and motioned.

From out of the woods came the rest of the killers, six in all. Billy Pardee and Decker were among them, but not their tall friend with the icy eyes, or Harvey, Keller's right-hand man. It was possible they had been shot, but Fargo couldn't recall seeing either take a slug. He watched as the man in the vest talked to Billy Pardee, who nodded and responded.

Climbing back on his horse, the man started up, his eyes on the ground. He was tracking them, Fargo realized, and wondered if maybe this was the same tracker who had used the lantern the previous night. Whoever the man was, he was good. He climbed slowly, warily, and when he was halfway to the top he palmed his pistol. There was a rifle in his saddle scabbard but he preferred the six-gun, which told Fargo more about him than an entire volume could.

Percy was as nervous as a kid in a dentist's office, fidgeting and moving his head from one side of the tree he was behind to the other side.

"Be still!" Fargo whispered.

The tracker's horse was giving him problems. It balked at the steep climb and had to be spurred. When it came to loose gravel that slid out from under its hooves, it stopped and refused to take another step. Accepting the fact, the tracker climbed down again and led the animal by the reins, skirting around the gravel.

Fargo could see the man more clearly now. He was in his late thirties, maybe early forties, with tanned, weathered features and a crook in the middle of his nose where it had once been broken. Pausing, the tracker waved an arm. Down below, Billy Pardee and the others began their ascent.

Fargo hadn't counted on this. He'd hoped the gunmen would be all bunched together, like geese in a pond. It changed everything. Somehow, he must dispose of the tracker without alerting Pardee and the rest. It would take some doing, but it could be done. Unfurling, he leaned the Henry against the pine, then slid the Arkansas toothpick out of its sheath. The miners and the accountant were watching him closely, apprehensive at the change in plan.

The man in the vest was taking his sweet time, stopping often to scrutinize the top of the ravine. He was suspicious, and rightfully so. But if he anticipated an ambush, he betrayed no fear, neither in his relaxed posture, nor in the casual manner in which he held his pistol at his side.

Appearances, as Fargo was all too aware, could be deceiving. The tracker was a coiled panther waiting to strike. Luring him in close enough to dispatch him with the toothpick would be like trying to lure a tiger into a cage.

Percy's nervousness was increasing by the moment. Now

he was cocking the derringer, then letting down the hammer, over and over and over again. At any second, the gun might go off.

Fargo gave him a stern glance and Percy stopped fidgeting. Gazing into the ravine, Fargo saw that the tracker had stopped again and was peering at the pines through narrowed eyes. Had the man seen something? Fargo wondered. Evidently not, for after a few seconds the gunman resumed climbing.

Lower down, Billy Pardee and the other cutthroats were leading their horses in single file. Decker was first, his hat pushed back, his shirt soaked with sweat.

The tracker only had twenty yards to go to reach the rim. Bending, he studied the ground with keen interest. When he straightened, he leveled his revolver, his thumb on the hammer.

Fargo figured the tracker would come up over the rim between Percy and himself. If the man spotted Percy first, which seemed likely, all it would take would be a few quick steps and Fargo could bury his toothpick to the hilt.

Fifteen yards away, now, the tracker's eyes continually flicked from tree to tree. His nickel-plated pistol glinted brightly in the sun.

Ten yards away, the man's horse dislodged a stone that rattled on down the slope. The horse stopped. Annoyed, the tracker jerked on the reins, never once taking his eyes off the trees.

At seven yards, the tracker was staring at the trunk that hid Percy Porter. The accountant was as rigid as a board, terror-stricken.

Fargo slowly pivoted so he would be facing the gunman when the man came over the rim. There would only be a second or two in which to act. Any delay would cost Percy his life; maybe Burns, as well.

The tracker only had five yards to cover, the steepest of all. He leaned forward, pulling on the reins, taking one long stride, then another. His head was almost as high as the rim. Another couple of yards would do it.

Suddenly, over by the boulder, George Prescott broke out in a loud coughing fit. Cynthia bent to stifle him but the harm had been done.

Percy Potter turned toward Prescott. In doing so, he showed himself. The gunman in the brown vest instantly fired, and crying out, Percy staggered, holding his shoulder.

Fargo was already in motion. He couldn't reach the tracker now without taking a slug. So, reversing his grip on the toothpick, he threw it just as he had countless times at countless targets. He could consistently embed it in a knothole the size of an apple at a dozen paces.

The tracker rotated, fanning his pistol, in the blink of an eye putting two shots into the tree Fargo had darted behind. The slugs thudded into the bark, barely missing him.

Fargo's throw was more accurate. The Arkansas toothpick sheared into the gunman's chest near the sternum. Grunting, the man took a partial step, blasting another bullet into the trunk. But the shot was squeezed off in pure reflex. The tracker was dead on his feet. Soundlessly, he keeled over, losing his hold on the reins.

That horse would come in handy. "Start shooting!" Fargo hollered as he snatched up the Henry. Bounding from concealment, he ran to catch the animal before it bolted. Lower down, the gun sharks sparked to life and commenced flinging lead up the slope. Pausing, Fargo fixed his sights on Decker. To compensate for the elevation, he raised the barrel a fraction, then fired. The Texan was lifted into the air by the impact and smashed into his mount. Like so much melted wax, he slumped to earth.

Titus and Burns had added their rifles to the din, as Burns cackled and shouted, "Give the devils hell!"

The tracker's bay was turning to run off. Fargo snagged the reins but was almost torn off his feet. Wrapping them around his left wrist, he sought to regain the bench before the gunmen picked him off.

Billy Pardee was bellowing like a madman, his words lost amid the roar of guns. Fargo surged upward, tugging with all his might. Bullets hit the ground all around him and the horse, and were smacking into the pines above. He didn't see how they would ever reach the rim safely, but they did.

"Hold on to these!" Fargo commanded, thrusting the reins at Porter, who was still upright, his stricken arm hanging limp. The accountant's throat bobbed and he leaped to comply, compelled as much by panic as anything else.

Fargo darted to a wide trunk and knelt. The gunmen had all found cover, a couple of them behind boulders, the rest retreating into the woods below. One of their mounts was down, kicking convulsively. A high-crowned hat appeared and Fargo sent it flying, its owner ducking low without snapping off a shot.

"Fargo!" Titus called, pointing to the right.

Burns was flat on his back, his limbs bent at awkward angles. Staying low, Fargo sprinted over and hunkered. A random shot had stained Burns's homespun shirt red, and the miner was breathing with great difficulty. Cynthia, ministering to Prescott, hadn't noticed.

"I'll get Cynthia," Fargo said.

"Don't bother." Burns's voice was a pale imitation of its former robust vitality. "I'm a goner. I'm all torn up inside. I can feel it." Drops of blood trickled from a corner of his mouth as he talked.

"I'm sorry."

Burns shook as if cold. "Just my dumb luck. It could have been any of you." Twisting his head, he pleaded with his eyes. "I have a favor to ask."

"Name it."

"Get word to my family. Tell my wife I thought of her at the end. Tell my kids I love them and—" Burns was racked by more shaking.

"I'll do it," Fargo said softly. "I promise you." The firing had stopped, and in the sudden stillness he heard Titus walk over.

"Never figured . . . to end . . . this way," Burns said. "Always thought . . . I'd die . . . down in the damn mine."

Titus placed a hand on his friend's shoulder. "Don't talk. Save your strength."

"For what?" Burns asked. It was the last thing he ever said. His eyes widening in surprise, he raised a hand toward the sky, sucked in a final breath, and was gone.

"He was a good man," Titus said, choked with grief. "I'm going to kill every last one of those sons of bitches for this. You see if I don't."

Cynthia came running over. She looked at Fargo, and he shook his head. "There was nothing you could have done."

"What about me?" Percy asked shrilly. "I'm shot and no one seems to care!" He was braced against the bay, as pale as a sheet, his left hand clasped to his right shoulder.

Fargo delayed long enough to take Burns's rifle, spare ammunition, and pocket knife. That was all the miner had on him.

Cynthia had moved the accountant over to the boulder near Prescott, and removed his jacket and shirt. The tracker had only winged Percy, the bullet searing a quarter-inch deep gash across his upper arm.

"You'll be stiff and sore for a week or so, but you'll live," Cynthia said, removing ointment and a small bandage from her bag.

"I've never been shot before." Percy had his face turned so he wouldn't see the wound. "For a while there I feared it was mortal. My whole life flashed before me, just like folks say it does. I remembered everything. A toy fire wagon I owned when I was six. A gold coin my grandfather gave me. The first ledger I owned. Everything."

"Your first ledger?" Cynthia said.

"It had my name engraved on the front, and the pages smelled like burnt wood. I used to sit and sniff them for hours at a time."

Maybe that explained a few things, Fargo reflected. "This is yours now," he announced, laying the rifle and ammunition down.

"Thank you, but I don't know what good it will do." Percy forgot about his shoulder and started to reach for the rifle, then flinched. "You saw me. I froze again, just like the first time. I'm worthless in a fight."

"Take it anyway," Fargo said.

Cynthia opened the ointment. "Do you think they'll keep after us?"

"Hard to say." Fargo had another important decision to make. With Prescott unconscious and the accountant being tended to, they weren't going anywhere for a while. Since he would rather not sit there and let their enemies bring the fight to them, he announced, "I'm going down."

Shoving the bottle of ointment into Titus's hands, Cynthia followed him. "Hold on. What do you think you're doing? If anything happens to you, the rest of us will never make it out alive."

"We need to know what they're up to," Fargo said, "and there's only one way to find out." He squeezed her hand to reassure her. "If I'm not back in an hour, put Prescott on the horse and circle back to the road."

Cynthia pressed up against him and pecked him on the cheek. "Be careful. I've taken a shine to you and I'd hate to see you come to harm."

"Makes two of us."

On the left side of the ravine, a huge boulder roosted just below the rim. Dropping on to his stomach, Fargo crawled down to it. Then, hugging the base, he snaked around to where he could scour the bottom without being spotted. Decker was sprawled where he had fallen, left to rot in the sun by his former partners. The dead mount was further down, still wearing its saddle. Of special interest to Fargo was the canteen that had been slung over the saddle horn and now lay near the animal's belly.

Fargo slid lower. They needed that canteen badly. The

water skin from the mud wagon had been entrusted to one of the guards who lost his life in the first gunfight. Presumably, Keller's men now had it.

By staying close to the ravine wall and availing himself of every boulder, rut, and bush, Fargo descended halfway down without incident. He heard no voices, and saw no one moving around. Which was just as well. The next twenty yards were barren of cover.

Fargo rose into a crouch. He could cross the clear area faster on foot than on his stomach. Girding himself, he launched into a run, zigzagging so he would be harder to hit. But no one tried. No shouts or gunshots echoed up the ravine.

Soon Fargo came to the bottom and wound through the vegetation, seeking sign. He didn't need to search long. Churned soil and a pool of blood marked where the gunmen had gathered after being driven off. Five separate sets of boot prints showed that one of them, possibly Billy Pardee, had paced back and forth, probably cussing and fuming while the wounded man was taken care of. Then all five had mounted and ridden northward, toward the road.

It appeared the gunmen had given up but Fargo had his doubts. Pardee wasn't the type to forgive and forget, and Decker had been a close friend of his. Then there was the mystery of Harvey's absence, and Luther Keller's whereabouts. Maybe instead of being driven off, Billy Pardee had gone for help.

Fargo climbed to the dead horse. A stray shot had smashed into its head above one eye, leaving an ugly hole. He slung the canteen over his left shoulder, then rummaged in the saddlebags to see what he could find. He struck a small bonanza consisting of half a pound of jerky, a box of .44 ammunition, and a shirt to replace the gore-soaked one George Prescott had on.

Hurrying upward, Fargo lingered long enough to un-buckle Decker's gunbelt and search the Texan's pockets.

Other than a wad of tobacco and a small roll of bills, Decker had nothing on him of worth.

Below the summit lay the tracker. Fargo yanked out the toothpick, wiped it clean on the dead man's shirt, and slid it into his ankle sheath. He also appropriated the tracker's gunbelt and revolver.

Cynthia, Percy, and Titus were all anxiously waiting, Percy gnawing on his lower lip as if it were a piece of venison. Their expressions asked the question uppermost on their minds.

"The gunmen have gone," Fargo said.

All three beamed. Cynthia clapped her hands, Percy giggled, and Titus let out a whoop.

"But they might come back," Fargo said, puncturing their elation. "Keller wasn't with them. Where he went is anyone's guess, but we know he won't rest until all of us are dead. Somewhere between here and the mine, his killers will try again."

"But for the time being we're safe enough," Cynthia said. "We can rest awhile. Have some of that jerky you brought."

Against his better judgment, Fargo gave in. "We'll stay for an hour. No more than that. In the meantime I'll rig up a travois for Prescott."

"A what?" Percy asked.

Fargo explained that certain Indian tribes relied on the travois to transport personal effects and haul lodges. It was a platform, fashioned by taking two long poles and securing them to the back of a horse, then lashing cross-braces between the poles behind the animal. Fargo had seen ones able to carry up to two hundred pounds or better. "Prescott is too weak to ride," he concluded. "A travois is the best way to move him."

Setting down the items he had collected, Fargo headed into the pines. "Help yourselves to a piece of jerky and a mouthful of water. No more than that, though."

"If you don't mind," Cynthia said, overtaking him, "I'd like to lend a hand."

"Aren't you hungry or thirsty?" Fargo himself wasn't, but only because he was accustomed to going without for long periods of time.

Cynthia averted her gaze. "I can eat later. I'm just too overwrought to sit still, is all. I need something to keep me busy."

"Then come along." Stopping, Fargo glanced back. Percy, licking his dry lips, was eagerly reaching for the canteen. "Remember—one mouthful. I know how much is in there so don't try to drink more."

The accountant frowned. "One measly mouthful? After all we've been through? It's inhuman."

"That canteen might need to last all of us for days," Fargo noted. "Take more than your share and you'll go without until we find more."

"I get the idea," Percy said testily. "What do you think I am, an imbecile?"

Fargo held his tongue and departed, winding through the tall trees in search of suitable limbs. He preferred to find branches that were on the ground since all he had to chop with was the Arkansas toothpick. Cynthia glued herself to his side. He tried not to think of the swell of her bosom or the sway of her hips but it was hard with her so close and the scent of her perfume so strong.

"May I ask you a question?"

"Sure," Fargo said, seeing a likely limb and walking over to inspect it.

"What are our prospects?"

"It depends. If we can circle back to the road without being bushwhacked, if Keller doesn't have any more surprises up his sleeve, if—"

Cynthia interrupted. "That's too many if's. Don't spare my feelings. Can you guarantee we'll live to reach the Silverlode?"

"There are no guarantees in life." Fargo liked the limb. It

was long and straight and only had a few thin offshoots to trim.

"That's what I was afraid you'd say." Cynthia walked in a small circle, wringing her hands. "I've never been in a situation like this before, never had to face the prospect of dying."

"You're holding up fine," Fargo said. He saw, though, that the strain of what they had been through was taking its toll. Cynthia looked tired and distraught, despite her lovely stoic countenance. To lighten her mood, he added, "A hell of a lot better than Percy Porter."

Cynthia smiled, then stood in front of him, her eyes aglow with a strange inner light. "I have something important to say. It's difficult, though. I'm not a forward woman."

"No one ever said you were." Fargo slowly rose, leaving the Henry on the ground. Something in her demeanor gave him a clue as to what she was about to say, but he told himself he was mistaken, that it couldn't be, that it was wishful thinking on his part.

"I want you—" Cynthia stopped, swallowed hard, and stared down at their feet. "I mean, I would very much like for us—" Again she stopped, unable to utter the crucial words.

Fargo tried to make it easy for her to back out gracefully. "Whatever is on your mind can wait. We've only got an hour and we have the travois to build."

"That won't take long," Cynthia said. Growing bolder, she inched forward until her bosom almost brushed his chest. "I'd like for you, I mean, for us, to, well, how do I put this without sounding like a common trollop?"

Fargo silenced her with a kiss. Her lips were soft and warm and sweet to the taste. As his tongue slid into her mouth, her tongue retreated, and she gave a tiny moan and clung to him as if she were about to faint. When they separated to take a breath, she leaned against him, panting.

"Why?" Fargo asked. More importantly, "Why now?"

"You'll think it's silly."

"Try me."

As Cynthia looked up, Fargo saw there were tears in her eyes. "I'm not a worldly woman, Skye. I can count the number of men I've been intimate with on one hand."

Fargo would need fifty hands. Or more.

"It's not that I don't like men. I do. Most just don't appeal to me. Those that have, well, let's just say I've enjoyed those intimate moments greatly. Does that make me shameless?"

"No." Fargo knew the feeling well.

"I don't want to die. That is, I don't want to die without feeling that special feeling one more time. And since I was smitten by you the moment I laid eyes on you, I thought maybe, just maybe, we could, ah, be together." Cynthia pressed a sleeve to her eyes to dry them. "I know what you're thinking. That I'm being ridiculous. That it's the stupidest thing you've heard in your entire life."

Fargo was thinking how delicious their kiss had been, and how much he would enjoy savoring her other charms.

"So if you don't want to do it, just say so. If I've made a complete and utter fool of myself, I apologize. I won't inflict myself on you any further."

Fargo pulled her to him, the feel of her full breasts sending a tingle through his body. "You talk too much," he said, and molded his mouth to hers.

10

Cynthia Howard was like a timid rabbit that wanted to venture from the safety of its warm burrow into the glaring light of day, but was afraid a coyote lurked in waiting to gobble it up. Plainly, she wanted Skye Fargo, she craved him, needed him to fill a burning hunger deep inside of her. But she was afraid to fully unleash her passion, afraid to let her emotions loose and enjoy the experience to the fullest. Her first few kisses were awkward, shy, reserved. She rested her hands on his broad shoulders, then kept them there as if fearful of roving any lower.

Fargo sensed her turmoil and acted accordingly. In the back of his mind a tiny voice warned they didn't have much time. They must fashion the travois and get out of there before the gun sharks returned. The tiny voice urged him to hurry, to do as Cynthia wanted and be done with it. But he knew that if he took her too quickly, too forcefully, it would scare and upset her, and might even result in her running off in tears.

So Fargo let their first few kisses linger. Their tongues entwined. He rimmed her gums with his, then delicately sucked on her lips one at a time. She closed her eyes and groaned loudly, her breath becoming hotter and hotter with each passing moment.

"No one has ever kissed me like you do."

Fargo slowly moved his right hand from her arm toward her breasts. A snail could move faster but he didn't want to spook her. When he cupped her breast, she issued a huge sigh of contentment and melted against him as if all the strength had fled her winsome form.

Becoming bolder, Fargo pinched the nipple. Cynthia arched her spine and dug her nails into his shoulders. He felt her nipple harden, felt her hot mouth nibble at his chin, his neck, his ear. She was beginning to give her carnal desire free rein. Lowering his mouth to her other breast, he covered it and breathed heavily, warming it through the material. Cynthia placed a hand on the back of his head and pressed him hard against her, bumping his hat off in the process.

"You make me giddy."

Fargo was going to do a lot more than that before he was done. He ran his left hand down her back to her shapely buttocks, massaging them briefly before sliding his fingers around to her thighs.

Cynthia gasped, and tensed.

Ever so slowly, Fargo caressed her upper legs, from her knees almost to her scorching mound. Calming her down was like calming down a champion racehorse, but the ride would be worth the effort. He caressed higher up, pushing on her dress, his forefinger brushing across her core. She shivered, then began to sink to the ground.

Looping his arms around Cynthia's waist and legs, Fargo lowered her to the grass. She was lovely beyond measure, her hair splayed like a reddish halo, her hem hiked up above her knees, her bosom rising and falling rhythmically. Something about the white dress lent her added sexual appeal.

"I know we don't have a lot of time—" Cynthia said.

"Enough." Fargo scanned the woods as he knelt. Other than several sparrows, there was no sign of life. Percy and the others were over a hundred yards away, well out of earshot. He bent down.

The risk they were taking was considerable, but Fargo could no more deny her than he could willingly stop breathing. Women were to him what gold was to others, what the

Silverlode Mine was to Prescott, what a quarter of a million dollars was to Keller.

Cynthia opened her mouth and her legs to him. His knee rubbed against her underthings as his hand undid enough of her dress to gain admittance to her ripe melons. He kneaded first one then the other, eliciting coos and sighs. When he took a taut nipple between his lips and rolled it around, she cried out and began to move her hips provocatively.

"So much," Cynthia breathed. "So much."

Fargo didn't need to ask what she was referring to. His right hand delved up under her dress, parted the sheer silken fabric, and brushed her moist slit.

"Ohhhhhhh!"

Fargo rubbed it, causing Cynthia to grab at him as if to pull him inside of her. She was ready, whether she knew it or not, and Fargo thrust his finger into her womanhood, clear to the knuckle. It brought her up off the grass, her thighs clamped tightly to his hips.

"Yes! Oh, yes!"

Fargo pulled his finger out and plunged it back in. He set a tempo, doing it again and again, each stroke having the same effect as adding a log to a bonfire. Cynthia's whole body was a glowing ember, her eyes blazing with pure lust. Her kisses now were molten lava, her hands had lost all their shyness.

Fargo found that out when his pants were abruptly opened and warm fingers enclosed his taut pole. It was so surprising, so pleasurable, and he stiffened at her touch. She ran her hand from top to bottom, provoking exquisite sensations.

"My, my. You're a rock."

What else did she expect? Fargo wondered. Inserting a second finger, he rammed them up into her. Cynthia let go of him, her mouth agape, her hips pumping into his hand.

"Ahhhhhh. Yesssssss."

Kissing her, Fargo slid his tongue across hers, then sucked on it as if it were sweet molasses. She sucked on his in return. Squeezing her right breast, he simultaneously swirled his fingers around and around inside of her.

"Soon?" Cynthia moaned huskily. "Please."

Fargo was thinking the same thing but for an entirely different reason. That tiny voice at the back of his mind would not stop railing about the monumental risk he was taking. At any moment, the gunmen might show up. Percy and Titus wouldn't stand a prayer.

"Oh, please, Skye."

Uncoiling, Fargo shoved his pants down, freeing his manhood. He slid his fingers out of her, then aligned his member and rubbed the tip over her glistening portal. Cynthia gripped him by the arms, her red lips formed into a delectable oval. He began to slide himself into her, inch by long, hard inch, until he was sheathed inside of her like a sword in its scabbard. For a minute they both were perfectly still, relishing the feeling.

"I'm ready," Cynthia said breathlessly.

So was Fargo. He rocked on his knees, slowly at first, in and almost out, in and almost out, the rocking movement becoming more pronounced as the impending explosion built. Their mouths fused. She rose to meet each of his thrusts, her ardor rivaling his, the slap of their bodies muffled by their clothes. They went faster and faster, harder and harder, until the trees were a blur and the ground shook and her lovely face was all Fargo could see, shimmering before him like a vision from a dream.

"Oh! Skye! Oh!"

Cynthia gushed, lifting both of them into the air with the violence of her release. Her legs were a vise, locking him to her. Not that Fargo had any inclination to pull away. He was close to the pinnacle himself. All it would take was a little prodding and he'd soar over the brink. The prod came in the form of Cynthia's hand, cupping his manhood. The contact of her fingers triggered his own eruption. Digging his fingers into her thighs, Fargo surged into her again and again. Her inner walls contracted around him in heavenly spasms. Cynthia was all velvet, all soft and yearning, and all woman.

It seemed to last forever. But the illusion was shattered as Fargo began to coast to a gradual exhausted stop. He sank on top of her, pillowed by her heaving breasts, his face nestled against her neck. Deep in her throat Cynthia made sounds like the mewing of a newborn kitten.

As much as Fargo would have liked to lie there for hours, he roused himself after a few minutes and rose onto his knees to hike up his pants and adjust his gunbelt. Cynthia's eyes were hooded, her mouth curled by a smile of total contentment. Languidly, she reached up and ran a finger along his jaw.

"I'd be the happiest girl alive if you were to treat me to a night on the town when we get back. What do you say?"

"First things first," Fargo said, imagining how upset Flora Flannigan would be if she saw him walking around Silver Flats with another woman on his arm. "Right now we'd better head back."

Pouting, Cynthia sat up and began arranging her clothes. "For a little while there I had forgotten all about our present nightmare." She wrestled with a difficult clasp. "I never did like Luther Keller very much but I'd never suspected he was capable of such heinous acts."

"Did he ever ask to take you on late night buggy rides?"

Cynthia looked up. "Why, yes. How did you know? He was forever badgering me about just that. Every time I went to the Silverlode, he'd hang around and pester me. Oh, he was always polite enough—he never grabbed me or anything. But the gleam in his eyes was enough to tell me what he was after."

Fargo roved in search of a dozen smaller branches and straight limbs that would suffice as cross-braces for the travois. It took longer than he liked but he found enough, and with them under one arm and one of the long poles under the other, he headed back for the shelf. Cynthia dragged the other long pole. Whenever he glanced at her she smiled coyly, a promise of future rapture stamped in her countenance.

Percy Porter had armed himself with a pistol and a rifle and was marching back and forth along the rim like an army private on sentry duty. "I'm loaded for bear," he declared as they emerged from the pines. "Next time I won't cower and quake." He puffed out his chest. "I'll blast those bastards to kingdom come."

Fargo would believe it when he saw it. He set about constructing the travois. Another hike down the ravine to the dead horse was necessary, in order to retrieve a rope he'd noticed on the saddle.

In half an hour the job was done. The bay balked at first, skittish at having the heavy travois fastened to its back. But after a while it calmed down and permitted Fargo to complete the work. He tested the platform by lying down on it. It wasn't exactly a feather bed, but it would do.

Titus helped Fargo lift George Prescott, then they looped rope around Prescott's chest and legs to hold him in place.

As Fargo was securing the last knot, Prescott's eyes opened. He tried to sit up, fear setting in when he found he couldn't. "What in the world?" he blurted, struggling. "Why am I tied up? What is going on?"

"Stay calm, George," Cynthia said, taking his hand. "You were shot, remember? I've bandaged you and put a new shirt on you and we're about to head for the mine."

Prescott glanced down at himself in confusion. Gradually, comprehension dawned on him and he sagged back. "I recall it all now. Luther! His despicable treachery. Turning against me, against the Anaheim Consortium."

"Calm yourself," Cynthia soothed. "You've lost a lot of blood. It wouldn't do to overexcite yourself."

"How can I stay calm at a time like this?" Prescott said. "Get me off this contraption! I don't like being strapped down. And I feel better than you give me credit for." He tried to struggle again, but a sudden bout of weakness made him slump and groan.

"See?" Grinning, Cynthia patted his chest. "Haven't you heard that doctors and nurses always know what's best? You can't walk under your own power. You're in no shape to ride, either."

Prescott attempted to lift his arms. "I don't like being helpless."

"We won't let anything happen to you." Cynthia placed her black bag on the travois beside him. "Rest now. I'll be at your side every minute from here on out."

Fargo took hold of the bay's reins and led them off to the northwest. Having the horse made their trek easier in one respect, but it hindered them in another. They had to stick to relatively open ground to avoid obstacles that might snag or jostle the travois. It was slow going. So many boulders, trees, and tangles had to be skirted that they took twice as long negotiating the next slope as they would have otherwise.

Fargo posted Percy at the rear with instructions to keep his eyes peeled. The accountant was all too happy to oblige. His new weapons had girded within him newfound confidence, and he kept stroking the rifle as if it were a lover. Every now and then he would draw the revolver and give it an awkward twirl.

They had gone over half a mile when Percy suddenly cried, "Hey, everyone! Look at me!"

Fargo glanced back, and sighed. Percy was spinning the pistol around and around on the end of a finger.

"Do you see? I'm a regular gunfighter! I bet I can flip it in the air and catch it like I saw a man do once." Tittering excitedly, Percy attempted to duplicate the feat, only instead of flipping upward, the revolver slipped off his finger and thudded onto his foot. Yelping, Percy grabbed his shoe and hopped up and down like a mad stork. "Lord, that hurt! I think I broke a toe!"

"It would serve you right," Fargo said. Here they were, fleeing for their lives from a pack of vicious killers, and

Porter was acting like a ten year old given his first firearm. "Keep the revolver in your holster. You might damage it."

Percy sank onto a small boulder and hugged his foot, on the verge of tears. "I'm in agony, and all you care about is the stupid gun? Have you no compassion?"

"Not for idiots," Fargo said, snapping on the reins.

For an hour they toiled higher, the terrain growing more and more rugged. They saw an eagle soaring high on the air currents, and spotted several elk far off. Jays screeched in the trees and ravens glided silently by. But they saw no one else until about the middle of the afternoon when Percy Porter hollered, "Look! I think we're being followed!"

That they were. Fargo counted three riders and a man on foot, over half a mile off but right on their trail. Which begged the question: Where were the rest of Keller's men? "They haven't spotted us yet. We'll keep moving."

"Can't we ambush them like we did before?" Percy asked. "I can't wait to put a bullet into one of those scoundrels."

This from the mouse who had been too timid to pull the trigger. Fargo shook his head. "They won't fall for the same trick twice. Don't shoot unless I say to."

"What a spoilsport," Percy complained. "I finally have an opportunity to prove my mettle and you won't let me."

"You'll get your chance," Fargo predicted. From then on he checked on their pursuers every couple of minutes. The quartet moved rapidly, guided by the man on foot, another tracker from the look of things. The man wore a black hat and carried a rifle. Fargo could tell little else at that distance, except that the new tracker might have on knee-high moccasins.

Ten minutes brought them to the flat crest of a ridge. While Cynthia gave Prescott water, Fargo stepped to the rim and was joined by Titus.

"I've been studying those fellers yonder and I might know something important." The miner pointed. "You see that jasper in the black hat?"

"What about him?"

"That could be Injun Charlie, a half-breed who works at the mine. Or, rather, *for* the mine." Titus elaborated. "We're always in need of fresh meat. So Injun Charlie and three or four others were hired by Mr. Prescott to bring us deer and elk whenever they can. Charlie's the best of the bunch. Hardly a week goes by that he doesn't fetch us something for the table."

"You're sure Prescott hired him?"

Titus's brow knit. "Now that I think on it, no. Luther Keller did. About a year ago, I reckon it was." He paused. "They say Injun Charlie is part Blackfoot or some such. Best damned tracker this side of the divide."

Just what Fargo wanted to hear. He scanned the ridge, another plan percolating. It might gain them a little time, and maybe even throw the gunmen off the scent until dark. "I want the rest of you to go on alone."

Cynthia was holding the canteen to Prescott's parched lips. "Whatever for? Isn't it wiser to stick together."

Fargo gave them the essential details. Titus nodded knowingly. Cynthia accepted it without comment. But the other two didn't like it at all.

"I must demand, in the strongest possible terms, that you stay at our side," George Prescott said. "Without you we're at the mercy of the killers, of the elements, of everything. I should have listened to you before but I was too damn stubborn. Now I've learned better. For all our sakes, don't leave us alone."

"It has to be done," Fargo said.

Percy was rubbing specks of dust off his rifle. "I don't mind that. I just don't think you should do it alone. Let me go with you. I won't get in your way."

To soothe the accountant's feathers, Fargo said, "I need someone I can depend on to protect Miss Howard." Turning, Fargo winked at her.

"And we need you to help watch over Mr. Prescott, Percy," Cynthia said. "Safeguarding him is more important than anything else."

Percy wasn't satisfied. "Sorry, Miss Howard, but I still need to prove something to myself. I realize you're trying to keep me from harm, but I survived the last time and I'll survive this time, too. Besides, there are four of them. Fargo will need me."

The accountant's help was the last thing Fargo needed. Porter had spoiled their first ambush and Fargo didn't want Porter to spoil another. "No. And that's that."

"How will I ever be able to demonstrate I'm not yellow?" Percy grumbled. "It's all I ask."

"You'll have plenty of chances later." Fargo gave charge of the bay to Titus, and the four of them began to trudge toward the dense forest. Cynthia smiled and waved, Percy bestowed a glance on him that would wither a cactus, and George Prescott stared somberly.

After they were out of sight, Fargo lowered himself onto his belly and over to a clump of weeds. Parting the stems with the Henry, he slid the barrel in among them. He saw the slope beyond clearly enough, but no one would be able to spot him.

Injun Charlie and the three gunmen ascended briskly, the half-breed hardly ever bothering to study the ground. Skilled as he was at wood lore, he didn't need to. A scuff mark or the random scrape of a hoof or the travois poles were enough to glue him to the scent, just as those bloodhounds the previous night had been locked on to the Ovaro's.

Fargo sighted down the barrel, waiting for the breed to come within range. One shot was all it would take, then he could hasten after the others. In four to five hours the sun would set, and they would be safe until morning. Unless Luther Keller had more hounds stashed somewhere.

Injun Charlie, as the miners called him, was even warier than the previous trackers had been. He seldom took his eyes off the crest of the ridge. Again and again he stopped to scour it. The three gunmen, none of whom Fargo recognized, rode close behind Charlie, rifles across their saddles.

By Fargo's reckoning the foursome were only three hundred yards away when Injun Charlie did a strange thing. He pointed his rifle skyward and fired twice, one shot right after the other. Then he continued on.

Fargo figured it was a signal. More gunmen must be searching the immediate area, he reflected, and had to be close enough to hear. But no answering shots resounded off the high peaks.

After covering another hundred yards, Injun Charlie did it again. He trained his rifle at the clouds and banged off two closely spaced shots. Tilting his head, he listened for a reply. Seconds dragged by, and just when Fargo was convinced the shots had been pointless, artificial thunder rumbled to the south, the result of two closely spaced shots from far off.

Even so, Fargo wasn't unduly worried. The second search party had to be the better part of a mile away. By the time they reached the ridge, Injun Charlie would be wolf bait, and Fargo would be long gone. Without their tracker, the gunmen would be hard-pressed to find him and the others. He centered the Henry's front sight on the half-breed's chest, aligned the rear sight, and waited.

Fargo was a firm believer in single-shot kills, whether shooting game for the supper pot or dropping an enemy. One was all it should ever take. Usually to the head, but the heart and lungs were equally good targets. Sadly, not everyone shared his outlook. Too many people were all too willing to blaze away, even when they didn't have a clear shot. Countless times, deer or bear or Indians were wounded and traveled for miles in acute torment, bleeding every step of the way, before they weakened enough for the person who shot them to catch up and put them out of their misery.

Fargo didn't believe in making anyone or anything needlessly suffer. Whether he was after a buck, a buffalo, or an enemy, he always went for the kill with his first shot. If it wasn't possible, if the animal or man wasn't completely visible, or the angle was wrong, or the sun was in his eyes, or any other factor, caused him to only wound rather than slay, Fargo invariably waited for a better shot.

Now the Trailsman waited for the half-breed to climb into his sights. He shut all other sounds and sights from his mind to concentrate on Injun Charlie to the exclusion of all else. Fargo noted the half-breed's gait and stride, how Charlie held his body, getting a feel for the man's pace and posture, just as he would with a deer or an elk.

The best hunters were always those who knew their quarry as well as they knew themselves.

Injun Charlie, though, was more alert than any animal. Coming to a flat spot, he paused and raised a hand over his eyes to shield them from the glare of the sun, which was on its downward arc and at Fargo's back. A thick mane of black hair hung from under Charlie's high-crowned black hat, which was decorated with beadwork. He wore a loincloth over striped pants and knee-high moccasins, just as Fargo had guessed.

One of the riders said something to the tracker and Charlie gestured sharply. Then he angled his rifle and squeezed off two more signal shots. This time, the answer retorts were closer.

Fargo hadn't moved a muscle. The slightest motion would cause the half-breed to seek cover. He stared down the Henry, patiently waiting as Injun Charlie veered wide of a deadfall and, exhibiting the agility of a cat, scrambled up and over a series of boulders. When Charlie straightened, the top of his hat rose into Fargo's sights.

The same rider yelled out again, and again Injun Charlie twisted. The two talked for a bit, and Fargo remained totally motionless the whole time. He thought of the horses the gunman had, and on the spur of the moment, he changed his plans. He'd only intended to stop their tracker, but now he decided to exterminate the entire bunch.

Injun Charlie faced the ridge and took another stride. His face filled the Henry's sights. Instantly, Fargo stroked the trigger. The rifle belched lead and smoke, the stock recoiling into his shoulder. At the same moment, Injun Charlie's head dissolved into a spray of crimson mist.

Rashly, the gunmen applied their spurs, rushing toward the crest, firing as they came. They were amateurs at their stock-in-trade or they would never have been so impetuous. Fargo only had to shift his elbow a fraction to bring the one on the right down. The other two didn't realize their compadre had fallen, they were so busy working their own rifles. Fargo planted a slug between the eyes of the man in the middle, then another in the sternum of the killer on the left.

Two of the three mounts trotted a short distance and stopped. The third raced almost to the top of the ridge before it, too, halted.

Fargo smiled and stood. Everything had worked out just fine. He heard shots and assumed it was the search party to the south. But when he bent his head back, he realized the sound came from the west—from the direction in which Cynthia and the others had gone. Suddenly, mingled with the crackling retorts, rose the piercing scream of a terrified woman.

11

Skye Fargo ran to the sorrel that had halted just below the crest. As he moved to climb on, the skittish horse pranced backward, refusing to let him mount. Another scream spurred Fargo into lunging for the bridle. Wheeling, the sorrel cantered off.

Left with no other choice, Fargo jogged toward the pair of horses lower down. The crash of gunfire lasted for another half a minute, long enough for him to get close enough to a black gelding to snatch its dangling reins. Vaulting into the saddle, he sped to the top and galloped hard on the trail left by his companions. Just before he entered the forest he looked to the south, and spied riders approaching fast.

There had been three search parties, Fargo realized, not two. One to the east, south, and west. There might be one to the north, too, for all he knew. Luther Keller was nothing if not thorough.

Scarcely slowing, Fargo threaded through the trees. He doubted the others had gone very far in the short time they'd had, certainly no more than half a mile. He soon learned that he was right.

The pines ended at a talus slope which Cynthia and Percy had wisely avoided. He stuck to their tracks, climbing into a belt of aspens. Ahead was a meadow. Rising in the stirrups, Fargo saw figures moving about. He promptly slowed to a walk, advancing until he was in peril of discovery, then he slid off and cat-footed to the edge of the trees.

Titus was dead. The miner was facedown in a spreading scarlet puddle, his arms outflung to his sides. Percy Porter had a bullet wound high in his right shoulder but he was alive, his wrists bound behind his back. George Prescott still lay on the travois, unharmed. As for Cynthia, she was being rudely groped by two men who had her by the arms.

Five of Keller's gun sharks were to blame. Their leader was Billy Pardee, and the young Texan was smirking in smug satisfaction. "You yacks should have listened to me and dropped your hardware when I told you." He nodded at Titus. "That lunkhead might be alive if you had."

Percy was trembling, whether from fear or fury Fargo couldn't say until the accountant opened his mouth. "If I hadn't froze we'd have driven you off."

"Who are you kiddin', pencil-pusher?" Pardee said. "You couldn't hit the broad side of a stable with a shotgun at two feet."

The other gunmen laughed. One shoved Cynthia onto her knees, another ran his fingers roughly through her hair.

"Hell, mister," Pardee told Percy, "if you had half the spunk this gal does, you'd be a regular terror."

"I tried to shoot you," Percy said, barely loud enough for Fargo to hear. "I really and truly did."

Pardee chuckled. "Don't feel bad. Anybody who can scream as loud as you can doesn't need a gun. You about punctured my eardrums."

So it had been Percy who had screamed, Fargo mused, not Cynthia. He wedged the Henry to his shoulder, then saw that one of the killers had pressed a cocked revolver to her head. On the man's right cheek were bloody scratch marks.

"Say the word, Tex, and this bitch dies."

"Now, now. Our uppity boss wants her alive, remember?" Pardee said. "Let's light a shuck, boys!"

"What about those other shots we heard?" another hardcase asked.

"That was probably Injun Charlie lettin' everyone know

he was on their trail. He'll show up at camp sooner or later. The same with Sheffield and his bunch." Pardee climbed onto his mount and extended his arm to Cynthia. "Up you go, lady. It'll be nice and cozy sharin' a saddle with you. Hell, by the time we get there, you and I will be the best of friends."

"Not in this life," Cynthia said.

Another gunman nodded at George Prescott. "What about him? And the greenhorn?"

Billy Pardee swung the nurse up behind him before replying. "Why are you fellas askin' me such godawful stupid questions? Keller wants Prescott alive, too, doesn't he? So we'll take him and the pencil-pusher both." Pardee chuckled. "Maybe we can get Porter to scream for Mr. Keller like he screamed for us."

A few well-placed rifle shots would drop half of them before they knew what was happening, but Fargo lowered the Henry and retraced his steps to the gelding. Putting an end to Pardee would give him considerable satisfaction but not nearly as much as putting an end to Luther Keller. As much as he wanted to help Cynthia and the others, he'd help them more by shadowing the Texan's party.

The gunmen were in good spirits, and not as vigilant as they should have been. They joked and laughed, Pardee loudest of all, spouting lewd comments about Cynthia and what they would enjoy doing to her.

Their destination was a stark peak to the southwest. Snow mantled its rocky summit and sparse timber dotted its lower slopes. Hours passed. Shortly after the sun dipped below the western rim of the world, blazing all of creation with vivid bands of red, yellow, and orange, Fargo spotted tendrils of smoke spiraling upward.

Because of all the open ground above, Fargo let Pardee get a sizable lead—there was little risk of losing them. Flickering fingers of flames pinpointed their exact location. Fargo went as close as common sense dictated on horseback, then ground-hitched the gelding and glided nearer, to a low earthen mound.

Fargo had found Luther Keller at last. Harvey was there, too. But the only gunmen were those who had been with Billy Pardee. It was Fargo's guess that Keller had sent out the three search parties, then sat around waiting for word. Now the mastermind was in front of the travois, hands on his hips, grinning at Prescott. His words carried clearly, each one laced with bile.

"So, George. It ends as I always knew it would. I've won. I can dispose of you at my leisure, then take over the Silverlode."

Prescott was pale from loss of blood. Sluggishly lifting his head, he attempted to spit on his former assistant, but missed. "Damn you, Luther! Damn you all to hell!"

"Don't be bitter, George. I'm not a sadist. Your end will be swift and painless. It's the least I can do for the man whose stupidity dumped a fortune in my lap. I'll think of you fondly in coming years. Whenever I go to the bank. When I'm in my mansion, being waited on hand and foot by servants. When I escort beautiful women in one of the finest carriages made."

Percy Porter was seated by the fire, a gunman holding a six-shooter on him. Still, he brazenly remarked, "Gloat all you want! You haven't won yet."

Keller turned to Cynthia Howard, who stood with her head held high in defiance. "Why does he make such a claim, my dear, when all of you are completely at my mercy?" Keller cupped her chin in his hand. "Tell me again about Fargo," he said suspiciously. "Tell me about his death."

Cynthia swatted Keller's arm aside. "There's not much to tell. Fargo was killed during a gunfight with Pardee and his men."

"So you would have me believe," Keller said, and rotated toward the young Texan. "Did you see Fargo's body, Billy?"

"No, sir. Me and the boys cut out. It was the smart thing to do, with Decker and Gantz dead, and Milt wounded." Pardee wedged his thumbs under his gunbelt. "I told you all this before, remember? Then you sent me out again and we caught these three."

"Never once seeing any trace of Fargo?"

"Sure didn't. Why are you so worried? He's just one hombre. Even if he is alive, we can lick him without half tryin'. Injun Charlie and Sheffield will be back before long, and the whole outfit can ride to that ravine tomorrow and verify her story. If she's lyin', Injun Charlie will track Fargo down."

Luther Keller made an exaggerated show of smacking his forehead. "Now why didn't I think of that? I should thank you, Billy, for sharing your profound insights." Abruptly taking several strides, Keller jabbed a finger into the Texan's chest. "I don't like loose ends, boy. I've made that abundantly clear time and again. And Fargo is a loose end." He poked Pardee once more. "When she told you he was dead, you should have sent someone to the ravine to check right then."

"I didn't think—" Billy began.

"No, you *didn't*," Keller hissed. "Nor does anyone else around here. Which creates no end of problems. I expect you to figure out some things on your own. Especially something as important as Fargo's whereabouts."

Pardee didn't like being jabbed. He bristled, about to respond, but Harvey materialized at Keller's elbow. Instead, the young Texan swallowed his pride and glowered.

Luther Keller stepped back, his thumbs hooked in his vest pockets. "Long ago, Billy, I learned an important lesson. A man must learn to control both his emotions and his tongue or he'll never amount to much. You, boy, have never learned to control either, and I doubt you ever will. Combined with your habit of always questioning my orders and talking back, it makes you more of a liability than an asset, as our accountant friend might say."

"I've lost your sign," Pardee said.

"Ah. Phrased more simply, I no longer have a use for you. In your parlance, you're free to light a shuck to parts unknown with no hard feelings."

"What about the money you promised? A thousand dollars for each man who rode with you."

"For each man who sees this through to the end," Keller clarified. "You, however, won't be. All you're entitled to are my sincere wishes for a prosperous life."

Billy Pardee lowered his hands. "What the hell are you tryin' to pull? You expect me to pull up stakes without enough money to my name to buy a cup of coffee? I spent all I had tryin' to find you."

"Then accept this as a token of my appreciation." Keller took a thick wad of bills out and peeled off a couple.

"Twenty lousy dollars?" Pardee said. "That won't last me to Denver. I want a hundred, at least."

"Twenty, and no more," Keller said, dropping the bills at his feet.

Pardee started forward, stopping when Harvey moved between them. "Now, you listen here, Mr. Keller. I lost two good friends on account of you. If you want shed of my company, fine. But I figure you owe me more than a measly pittance." When Keller simply stared, Pardee went rigid with anger. He deliberately held his hands out from his hardware, then started to bend to pick up the money.

"I knew you would be reasonable," Luther Keller said in a mocking tone.

"Texans know better than to buck a stacked deck," Pardee said, twisting slightly, his right hand casually dipping to the butt of his Remington.

Keller didn't seem to notice. "Really? Evidently no one thought to inform Travis, Bowie, and Crockett at the Alamo. Or Sam Houston at San Jacinto. Texans are as foolishly spirited as mustangs, I've found."

"Then you should know better than to poke and prod one," Billy Pardee said. With that, the freckle-faced hellion slapped leather. He was ungodly quick, chained lightning in human guise. His Remington flashed up and out almost too swiftly for the human eye to follow. Anyone who blinked missed it. Just as they missed what Harvey did, which was to whip out his own ivory-handled Smith & Wesson as if plucking it from thin air.

Two shots boomed almost simultaneously. Billy Pardee fanned his pistol twice more but his slugs plowed into the earth beside Harvey's boot. Taking a single stride, Pardee sought to straighten his arm to fire again, but he couldn't. Surprise contorted his freckles as his legs gave out and he sank in a disjointed heap.

Harvey lifted the Smith & Wesson to his lips and blew at the smoke curling from the barrel. "The kid was fast, boss," he said. "Mighty fast."

"But a pain in the ass," Keller said. "One minute he was licking my boots, the next he was arguing over trifles."

"Texans," someone said. "They're a contrary bunch, ain't they?"

None of the gunmen, Fargo noted, seemed particularly upset about Pardee's death. By the same token, none of them seemed particularly pleased, either. It didn't take a genius to figure out why. They were thinking that the same fate might befall them if they dared to buck Keller.

As far as Fargo was concerned, they could go on gunning each other down until there weren't any left. Each one of them who ate lead made it that much easier for him to rescue Cynthia, Percy, and George Prescott.

Speaking of which, while two of the gun sharks dragged Billy Pardee over by the horse string, Luther Keller walked up to his former boss. "Now where were we? Ah, yes. I was extolling the virtues of being filthy rich. What do you think? A summer home in St. Louis and a winter home in New Orleans?"

"I pray you rot in perdition," Prescott said. The mere act of speaking took terrific effort, and when he was done he closed his eyes and groaned.

"I should think you'll be there before I will," Keller said. "But look at the bright side. From what I hear, the weather down there is constant the year round." Keller snickered. "It's hot as—dare I say it?—hell."

The gunmen cackled.

Percy Porter waited for their mirth to fade, then interjected, "It's easy to impress simpletons, isn't it?"

"You should know," was Keller's rejoinder. "I'd watch my tongue, were I you, accountant. The only reason you're still alive is the amusement you'll afford us tomorrow when we put you to the test."

"What test?"

"Putting a bullet in your brain would be too easy, too dull," Keller informed him. "I have something special in mind."

Percy didn't know when to leave well enough alone. "Does your mother know she gave birth to the rottenest son of a bitch who ever drew breath? Or do you even *have* a mother?"

Luther Keller wasn't amused. He nodded at Harvey, who palmed the Smith & Wesson, reversed his grip, and struck Percy across the temple, knocking him into the dirt. Cynthia leaped to his aid but another gunman grabbed her and wouldn't let go, even though she struggled her utmost.

"Any more insults from you, accountant," Keller growled, "and Harvey will pound on your skull until it's mush. I trust I've made myself clear?"

Fargo had listened to enough. Slanting to the left, he circled the camp. His plan was to spook their horses, then in the general confusion spirit Cynthia and the others out of there. As plans went it left a lot to be desired, but he couldn't think of anything better and he didn't have all night. The third search party, the one led by the gunman named Sheffield, might show at any second.

A sharp smack stopped Fargo in his tracks.

Percy, incredibly, had risen to his knees and said something that earned him a vicious slap from Keller.

"Go ahead. Beat on me all you want," Porter said, blood trickling from his split temple. "I still say you're the worst bastard who ever drew breath."

At a gesture from Keller, two gunmen gripped Percy by either arm and hoisted him erect. Keller slapped him again, but lightly this time, toying with him. "That rap on the skull must have jostled your brain. In case you haven't noticed, I hold your life in the palm of my hand. One word from me and your wretched existence ends."

"I don't care," Percy declared, and the wonder of it was, it truly sounded as if he didn't. "I'm not afraid anymore. I can prove it, too. Face me man-to-man, mister. I'll shoot you just like your filthy killer shot Pardee."

Fargo moved closer. The accountant had picked the worst possible moment to grow a backbone. Any one of the gunmen would drop him where he stood if Keller so much as snapped a finger.

"You will, will you?" Luther Keller said, and laughed. "I'll tell you what. How about if I give you the opportunity?" He glanced at a bearded underling. "Thomas, cut him loose and give him your revolver. Harvey, be so kind as to lend me yours."

A knife blade glistened, streaking once, twice, and then the rope that bound Porter fell. He swung his hands in front of him, grimacing in anguish. "My arms. . . ."

Percy's circulation had been cut off, Fargo deduced. That, and the wound in Percy's right shoulder meant a snail could unlimber a gun faster than he could. It was why Keller had accepted the challenge; it was one he knew he couldn't lose.

Cynthia recognized the same fact. "Percy, don't! Please! It's not a fair fight. You're hurt. You can't possibly beat him."

"Besting him isn't important," the accountant said. "Showing I'm not a coward is what counts."

Fargo stalked toward the ring of firelight. In his pain and fatigue, Percy wasn't thinking straight. Even if by some miracle Percy won, even if he demonstrated true courage by standing up to Keller, no one would ever know. Harvey or another gunman would put a slug into him before Keller's body hit the ground.

Thomas shoved a revolver into the accountant's left hand. Percy switched it to his right, wincing at the discomfort the slight movement provoked.

George Prescott had regained enough strength to raise his head. "Is there no end to your evil, Luther? You're a bottomless well of wickedness. Curse me for not recognizing your true nature sooner."

"Spare me the 'holier than thou' lecture," Keller responded. "It's easy for you to act so high and mighty when you make twice the salary I do. I'm no different than most people. In the greater scheme of things, the only one who matters to me is *me*."

"There's more to life than money," Prescott said.

"Wrong. Money is everything." Keller gazed into the distance. "Being poor is wretched. Obviously you've never had to go without meals, never had to wear rags for clothes, or scrounge in refuse." He looked at Prescott. "Being rich, on the other hand, allows us to live in the lap of luxury. So be honest with me, George. Which would any sane person prefer?"

Percy tried to extend the revolver, but found he couldn't. He raised it halfway, then his arm began to shake as he strained to hold it up. He gave up with a low groan.

"Something wrong?" Keller bated him. "Perhaps you should hold it with both hands." He accepted Harvey's Smith & Wesson. "This will be a first for me. I've never shot anyone before."

The stocky gunman had let Cynthia go since she had calmed down. Stepping up to Keller, she gripped his sleeve. "Please, Luther. I'm begging you. Don't do this, for my sake. If I've ever meant anything to you—"

"You haven't," Keller said bluntly.

"But what about all those times you asked me to go on buggy rides with you?" Cynthia brought up.

"How shall I put this, my dear?" Keller leered at her. "Men have urges we can't deny. You were a means to an end, a way for me to release my urge, but you always refused. So don't presume to impose on me now."

Cynthia hauled off and struck a solid blow to the jaw that snapped Keller's head back.

The stocky gunman, cursing luridly, leaped up to wrap his brawny arms around Cynthia, pulling her away. Harvey also sprang up, elevating a fist, but Keller grabbed his wrist.

"No. Don't bother. There are better ways to make her pay—to humiliate her."

Fargo stepped into the ring of firelight. No one had noticed him yet, but they did when he thumbed back the Henry's hammer. Out of pure reflex several gunmen spun, fingers clawing for their irons, but none of them were foolhardy enough to try and draw. He had the rifle trained on Luther Keller, who displayed no surprise.

"Well, well. I was wondering when you would put in an appearance. That story about your death didn't wash."

"No one move," Fargo warned, and let it go at that. All of them understood the consequences.

Harvey wanted to, though. Fargo saw it in the swarthy killer's eyes. But Luther Keller had Harvey's ivory-handled pistol. All Harvey could do was glare and clench his fists.

"My men won't lift a finger against you unless I order them to," Keller said. He oozed self-confidence, as if he were still in control of the situation. "Allow me to thank you, on their behalf, for saving them the trouble of hunting you down."

Percy showed all his teeth in a twisted grin. "What are you waiting for, Fargo? Shoot him! Shoot him so full of lead he'll look like a sieve!"

Keller sniggered derisively. "He can't, you pathetic dolt.

I'm the only thing keeping you and your friends alive. Slay me and my men will kill every last one of you."

There was Fargo's dilemma, in a nutshell. "Cynthia, I want Percy and you to lead the sorrel out of here. Head northeast. I'll be along in a bit."

The nurse started to comply.

"Not so fast," Keller said. "You honestly don't believe I'll allow you to just leave, do you? Even if I did, how far would you get dragging Prescott? In the morning we'll track you down in no time and finish it once and for all."

Fargo took another step. "Your men won't come anywhere near us."

"Oh? And why is that?"

"Because you're coming with us."

Keller wasn't pleased by the prospect. "You're only postponing the inevitable. You'll never reach town, not with George in the shape he's in."

"There's always the mine," Cynthia said. "They must have men out looking for us by now."

Luther Keller's grin was demonic. "I'm afraid not, my dear. I sent a rider to the Silverlode with word the mud wagon broke down with a cracked wheel. But they're not to worry. They were told that we'll have it fixed by morning and that the wagon will arrive by noon."

"Do you expect them to believe that?" George Prescott asked.

"Why wouldn't they?" Keller rejoined. "I sent Zeb. They know he runs errands for me. He's to say that I was on my way there on horseback when we came upon the mud wagon at the side of the road, and that Harvey and I stayed to help."

"How will you explain our deaths?" challenged Cynthia.

"Quite easily. After the wheel was repaired, Harvey and I headed for the mine. We heard gunfire and rode back to investigate. The wagon had been attacked by a band of outlaws, the money stolen, and everyone on board was slain or missing."

"You have it all worked out, don't you?" Prescott spat in disgust.

Keller chortled. "Yes, I do. I think of every contingency and plan accordingly. Fact is, I'll make an outstanding manager. The Anaheim Consortium won't miss you one bit, George. Eventually they'll want to promote me, but by then I'll have amassed enough silver to retire. I'll have servants to wait on me hand and foot. A carriage fit for a king. Meals served on the best china. My clothes made by the best tailors. Mansions in St. Louis and in New Orleans—"

"You've crowed about this before," Cynthia reminded him.

Fargo stiffened. Yes, Keller had, and it was strange he would do so again. It wasn't like Keller to prattle on. Unless he had a reason. Unless he was talking to distract them, to keep them focused on him so they wouldn't notice something—or someone—else. Fargo began to pivot but he had divined the true purpose too late.

"Don't even think about it!" a gruff voice commanded.

Four more gunmen, all with rifles, strode into the firelight, covering Fargo and the others. In the forefront was a hardcase in a long woolen coat and badly scuffed boots. "Sorry we're late gettin' back, Mr. Keller. We saw this feller holdin' a gun on you and snuck in on foot."

"No apology needed, Mr. Sheffield," Luther Keller said. "Your timing is perfect. Now we can get on with the business of killing these buffoons once and for all."

12

"Don't blame yourself," Cynthia Howard whispered. "I didn't see them sneaking up on us, either."

Skye Fargo did blame himself. He couldn't help it. Keller had duped him with one of the oldest ruses known. He had been unforgivably careless. Now the nurse, the accountant, and the mine manager would pay for his oversight with their lives. Prescott was still on the travois but the rest of them were seated by the fire, half a dozen gun muzzles staring them in the eyes.

Luther Keller rocked back and forth on his heels, hands behind his back, wearing a smirk as wide as the Mississippi. "It ended as I always knew it would. Now the question is how to dispose of you?"

"Give us the woman," Sheffield suggested. "Me and the boys will take her into the weeds. Toward mornin' we'll strangle her and bury her so deep, she'll push up daisies in China."

"Only if you gag her so she can't scream her lungs out," Keller said. "That leaves the other three. Prescott is mine. No one is to lay a finger on him. I want the pleasure of killing the jackass myself."

Fargo had a single ray of hope. He wasn't the only one who had made a mistake. The gunmen had neglected to look in his boots. But what good was one knife against almost a dozen men armed with guns? He scanned the camp, desperate for a means of saving himself and the others. He looked at the horse string, spotted saddles and bedrolls, saw the strongbox off to the right and the water skin lying near it. His glance shifted back to the strongbox and an idea popped into his head. It was a loco idea, but the only one he could think of.

"That leaves these other two," Sheffield said. "I reckon I'll do the honors." He sighted down his Spencer at Percy.

Fargo quickly put his plan into effect. "Go ahead. Get it over with. I just wish I could be here to see your faces."

Sheffield hesitated, lowering the rifle a fraction. "Our faces?"

"All the trouble you've gone to, all the work you've done for Keller, and for what?" Fargo hoped his laugh sounded genuine. "For nothing."

"What are you going on about?" Sheffield snapped.

"The money." Fargo pointed at the strongbox. "Keller promised all of you equal shares in the payroll, didn't he? It's why you hired on, isn't it?"

"Yeah. So?"

"So there *is* no money. Prescott and I filled the strongbox with sacks of rocks before we left Silver Flats. None of you will get a cent."

Sheffield jerked the Spencer down. "If that's true, I'll carve out your tongue and make you eat it, so help me God."

"See for yourselves," Fargo advised. "Then ask your boss how he intends to pay you. It'll take months for him to get up the money on his own."

The gun sharks stared at Luther Keller. "Even if it's the truth," he said, "all of you will get what's owed you. Trust me. I'm a man of my word. No one will ride off empty-handed."

"Tell that to Billy Pardee," Fargo remarked.

Sheffield looked around. "Say, where is that ornery Texan, anyhow?"

Fargo draped his arms across his knees, his hands hanging near the tops of his boots. "Your boss had him killed for wanting his fair share of the payroll."

"That's not quite how it happened," Keller said.

The next moment they were all talking at once, the gunmen who had been in Sheffield's search party demanding to know what had happened to Pardee while the gunmen who had witnessed the Texan's death tried to explain. Luther Keller sought to justify the deed to Sheffield while Harvey stood to one side, his hand on the Smith & Wesson.

Fargo and the others had been momentarily forgotten, just as Fargo had wanted. He slipped his fingers into his right boot, pulled the knife from the sheath, and slid it up his sleeve just far enough so no one would notice.

"I want the strongbox opened," Sheffield announced loud enough to be heard over the hubbub.

"So do I!" another hardcase exclaimed.

"Me, too!"

Keller held his arms aloft to calm them down. "All right! All right! If that's what you want, that's what you'll get." He walked to the travois. "Where's the key, George? We searched the pockets of the driver and the shotgun rider but neither had it."

"I don't have it either," Prescott said.

"You're lying."

"You know me better than that, Luther. I hid it in the mud wagon in case we were stopped. You'll have to send someone to fetch it."

Sheffield and most of the hired killers weren't inclined to wait. Surrounding the strongbox, they began pounding at the lock with rocks. Keller tried to dissuade them but they refused to heed. Sheffield pushed the rest away and set to work with determined vengeance, smashing the lock over and over again.

Everyone was watching, eager to learn what was inside, including Cynthia, Percy, and Prescott. Only one gunman continued to cover them, and he had turned sideways in order not to miss anything.

Fargo was the lone exception. Bending down, he whispered in Cynthia's ear, then he leaned to the left and did the same with Porter. They nodded to confirm they understood what they must do.

The cutthroats were clustered close around the strongbox, Keller and Harvey among them, Sheffield grunting with every blow struck.

Slowly, cautiously, Fargo eased up into a crouch. He had to be ready when the right moment came. The toothpick was close to his leg where no one would spot it.

"Damnation! It's taking forever!" Sheffield stamped a boot like a mad bull. "Find something harder for me to hit it with, boys."

"There ain't nothing harder," one man said. "We don't have any hammers or sledges handy."

"Hold on!" Sheffield shouted. "It's starting to give! Another minute should do it."

Everyone edged nearer. The man covering Fargo rose onto his toes to see over their shoulders. He was off guard and off balance.

Fargo surged upward, plunging cold steel between the gunman's ribs even as his other hand closed over the man's mouth to stifle any outcry. The gunman sagged without so much as a whimper and Fargo lowered him the rest of the way, taking his Remington. Then Fargo motioned to Cynthia and Percy. They rose and crept toward the sorrel to carry out their part of the plan.

The gunmen were pressed so close together Fargo couldn't see Sheffield. He stripped the dead man's gunbelt off and retreated toward the travois. The back of Luther Keller's head made a tempting target. He didn't shoot, though. The other nine would return the favor and gun down Cynthia, Percy, and Prescott as soon as Fargo fired.

At the next resounding blow, Sheffield yelped as if he had mashed his finger and declared, "The damn rock broke! Someone give me another!"

Fargo tensed. When they turned they were bound to see him. But another hardcase had a jagged rock already in his hand.

"Here. Use this one."

Quickening his pace, Fargo flanked the sorrel as Cynthia and Percy led it toward the encircling wall of darkness. The thud of the horse's hooves wasn't loud enough to be heard above the racket Sheffield and his band were making. Within seconds the night enfolded the escapees in its inky gloom as Cynthia clucked to the sorrel so it would go faster.

They crept ten yards. Twenty. Suddenly the crisp mountain air was shattered by whoops and hollers. Fargo saw the gunmen all move forward as the strongbox lid was thrown open.

"I'll be switched! The money's there after all!"

"I never saw so many bills and coins in all my born days!"

"And it's ours, boys!" Sheffield roared. "All ours!"

Fargo turned toward Cynthia. "No matter what happens next, don't stop. I'll hold them off as long as I can, then I'll catch up." She slowed, reluctant to comply. "Go," Fargo insisted. "Save Prescott."

Percy tugged on the sorrel's bridle. "You heard him. Come on. They'll notice we're missing any moment."

In the very next second, an outraged bellow brought all the gunmen around to gaze in befuddled astonishment at the empty space by the fire where their captives had been. Luther Keller shoved through the group, glanced at where the sorrel should be, and uttered a snarl worthy of a mountain lion.

"After them! Find them! Kill them on the spot! Every damn one of them!"

"Even the woman?" Sheffield asked.

"All of them!"

Every hardcase except Harvey ran toward the horse string. Fargo brought the Remington to eye level and banged off two swift shots. A man fell at each thunderous roar. The rest either dived flat or whirled and replied with hot lead.

Fargo threw himself onto the ground as the darkness was blistered by buzzing lead. His next bullet smashed into the forehead of a gunman rushing toward him.

"Shoot at his muzzle flash!" Sheffield hollered.

Fargo rolled to the right, not once but three times. He heard the *thup-thup-thup* of rounds hitting the spot where he'd just lain. Again he fired, his shot penetrating the shoulder of a killer taking careful aim.

"He's moved!" Sheffield yelled.

Fargo wished he had the Colt. He'd used it for so long, it was as much a part of him as his hands and feet. Sighting with it was instinctive, automatic. The heavier, longer Remington felt unwieldy by comparison. He knew frontiersmen who favored Remingtons, using them as skillfully as he did the Colt, but they were accustomed to the model. He wasn't.

Sheffield started to rise. "Up and at him, boys! He can't stop all of us at once!"

No, but Fargo could stop Sheffield, and he did, shooting him in the chest, going for the heart. Unfortunately, Sheffield moved just as Fargo squeezed the trigger and the shot caught him high on the shoulder.

Pushing upright, Fargo ran, replacing spent cartridges on the fly. Rampant confusion gripped the gunmen, some shouting they should give chase, others wary of running pell-mell into the night, still others checking on those who had fallen. It was left to Luther Keller to seize command. Storming among them, he barked orders. Everyone who could ride, including Sheffield, was told to mount up.

Fargo had whittled the odds down some. Counting Keller and Harvey, he had seven badmen to deal with. But he had lost the element of surprise. They also had horses and rifles, and he didn't. He had to rely on his wits to make up the difference.

Since Cynthia and Percy had been bearing eastward, Fargo changed direction, sprinting to the north to lure the gang away. He kept glancing back, and when they had climbed on their mounts and began racing after him in pursuit, he stopped, adopted a two-handed grip to steady the Remington, and stroked the trigger twice.

Sheffield took two more slugs, this time lower down in his chest. Flinging his arms overhead, he pitched into eternity.

"There!" Keller bawled. "That way!"

Fargo ran flat out as the night erupted with the crack of pistols and the blast of rifles. Bullets zipped by on both sides. One nicked his hat. Another clipped a whang under his right arm. Another nearly took off an ear. The gunmen were spreading out, with Luther Keller and Harvey in the center. They didn't know exactly where Fargo was but they had a good enough idea and were flinging enough lead to riddle a dozen men.

Suddenly throwing himself to earth, Fargo twisted to face his pursuers. The firing had tapered off as several gunmen scoured the area, others reloading their weapons.

Keller was standing in the stirrups, peering right and left, a study in frustration. "Where the hell did he go?"

"He has to be here somewhere, boss."

Fargo pointed the Remington at Keller. One shot would end it. Without their leader the rest would disperse, except maybe for Harvey, but Fargo would deal with him when the time came. Fargo smiled grimly as his thumb curled around the hammer, applying pressure. The slight click wasn't heard by the hardcases. He went for a head shot, the pull of his finger clean and quick.

Nothing happened.

Puzzled, Fargo tried again. Once more the gun failed to fire. He knew there were unused cartridges in the cylinder so it wasn't that the revolver was empty. It had to be a malfunction—either the firing pin had broken or something else was wrong. Whatever it was, it left him with no weapon.

The gunmen were rapidly coming closer.

"Anyone who spots him, call out," Luther Keller instructed them.

"Before or after we make wolf bait of him?" someone responded.

The gun sharks were spaced apart at ten- to twelve-foot intervals, not nearly enough for Fargo to avoid discovery when they went by. Setting the spare gunbelt down, Fargo snaked to the right a couple of yards, enough to put him midway between two riders.

"See anything?" Keller impatiently demanded.

The two men bearing down on Fargo weren't looking at the ground. They were doing what everyone else was doing, namely, staring off into the darkness. Fargo concentrated on the man on the right, since wedged under the man's belt was Fargo's Colt. He aimed to get it back.

"Damn it! " Keller fumed. "He can't have gone far!"

Fargo rolled onto his side, crooked his arm, and tossed the Remington at Luther Keller's mount. The horse whinnied and reared, and every gunman spun around to see why.

Exactly as Fargo planned. He heaved upward, gripped the gunman's leg, and wrenched the man's boot from the stirrup, pushing with all the considerable power in his broad shoulders and muscular arms.

Yelping, the gunman toppled and was unhorsed. Fargo moved around the man's mare in the blink of an eye, his foot connecting with the gunman's mouth as the cutthroat attempted to rise. His teeth shattered, the gunman pitched onto his backside. Frantic, the killer stabbed for his revolver but his speed wasn't the equal of Fargo's.

In a blur, Fargo yanked the Colt from under the man's belt, pressed the muzzle against his gut, and fired. The gunman screamed, doubling over as Fargo straightened and spun. The next hardcase had swiveled and was raising a rifle. Fargo fanned the Colt twice, the slugs punching him backward into thin air.

Now all the gun sharks knew where Fargo was, and wheeled their animals toward him. Not Luther Keller, though. He couldn't bring his horse under control. Between being struck by the Remington and the shots and screams, the animal was in sheer panic. With Keller hauling on the reins to no avail, the horse raced off.

The darkness flared with flashes of flame. Fargo responded to the nearest, then pivoted, stepping closer to the mount of the man he'd just shot, keeping it between him and those seeking to kill him. Fingers flying, he reloaded, a feat he had done so many times he could do it with his eyes shut if need be. He snapped the loading gate down and burst out from behind the mare, his Colt blazing.

A burly gunman was almost on top of him. Fargo fired, dodged the man's onrushing horse, then turned toward another rider and fired again. One man went down but the other didn't. More flames stabbed the night. Each was answered in kind.

Suddenly the booming ceased. All was still. Fargo reloaded again, listening to the nicker of a horse and the moans of a dying man. He had lost count of how many he had shot, of how many were left. Harvey was unaccounted for, he knew that for sure. Plus Keller, wherever he had gotten to.

The moans grew louder. Fargo waited, motionless as a tree. Other than the breeze, nothing stirred. He then walked over to the wounded gunman and added another hole to the one already in the man's chest.

The mare hadn't moved. Fargo slowly moved toward her, wary of taking a slug in the back. He gathered up her reins and forked leather, heading in the direction Cynthia and Percy had gone. In a quarter of an hour, he overtook them.

Percy had found a dead limb and brandished it like a club as Fargo approached. "Who's there?" he challenged. "Stay back or I'll bash in your skull!" He waved the branch overhead, then grinned sheepishly when he recognized the Trailsman's form. "Oh! It's you! We heard a lot of shooting and feared you were dead."

Fargo climbed down to check on Prescott and gave them a brief account. George was unconscious, but he'd stopped bleeding and his pulse was strong, which Cynthia took as a good sign.

"I'll never be able to thank you enough for what you've done," she said, placing a hand on his elbow. "My invitation to a night on the town still holds."

Staring into her lovely eyes, filled with so much warmth and promise, Fargo found it impossible to come right out and decline. "We'll see how things work out."

"Where to now?" Percy inquired. "Back to the road? Or do we head overland to the mine?"

"We're going to Keller's camp," Fargo said.

The accountant took a step back. "Is that wise? Didn't you say Luther and Harvey got away? They might be there, waiting for us."

Fargo doubted it. Keller wouldn't expect them to go back there, for one thing. For another, it was too dangerous for the pair to stick around. No amount of money was worth being lynched. Soon the miners would know of Keller's scheme, and they were liable to string them both up on sight. Fargo figured Keller would get shed of Silver Flats just as fast as his horse could carry him.

Still, Fargo took precautions. When the dying glow of the campfire in the distance alerted him that Keller and Harvey were close, he made the others wait while he went ahead alone. The bodies of those he had shot lay where they had fallen. Three horses had been left behind, along with a trio of saddles and bedrolls—and the strongbox. But Fargo hadn't returned specifically for them. Propped on one of the saddles was his motive—the Henry. Hollering for Cynthia and Percy, he saddled two of the mounts—one for her, and one for himself. The accountant would ride the mare.

George Prescott had come around and was sipping from the canteen. "I'll live," he said when Fargo asked how he was feeling. "Thanks to you. If there's ever anything I can do on your behalf, say the word."

"There is one thing."

"Name it."

"The miners who died protecting the payroll—" Fargo was thinking especially of Titus and Burns. "Some left wives and families. They could use a little money to tide them over. Say, six months' wages."

"Consider it done."

After tying a lead rope on the sorrel, they prepared to leave. Cynthia and Percy gave Fargo a hand lifting the strongbox onto the travois. Fargo was half afraid the combined weight of Prescott and the box would cause the sorrel to balk, but the horse didn't act up. For hours they forged northward, and it was close to midnight when Fargo called a halt. By then Percy could barely sit the saddle, his wound and the beating he'd suffered taking their toll.

The night was quiet. Fargo stood guard alone, the others too exhausted to share the responsibility. Thanks to a can of Arbuckle's, a bundle of jerky, and a coffeepot and cups he found in one of the saddlebags, he had breakfast ready just as dawn painted the eastern sky in spectacular colors.

Cynthia, Percy, and Prescott were so happy to be alive, their smiles competed with each other to see which one showed the most teeth. Prescott had recovered enough to sit up. Percy's shoulder was sore and his arm was stiff, but he could move it better than he had the previous night. Cynthia couldn't stop giving Fargo inviting looks, which he pretended not to notice.

It was about nine in the morning when they reached the rutted road and turned westward. Cynthia was humming to herself as Prescott dozed in the saddle. They came to a sharp switchback and wound slowly up it onto a bluff. Fargo was in the lead so he was the first to see the two figures waiting in the middle of the road. He had to admit he was surprised to see them, and he commented as much as he drew rein.

Luther Keller sneered in contempt. "You expected me to run off like a whipped dog with my tail between my legs? If that's the case, you underestimate me."

Fargo slid down, turning so his back wouldn't be to them. "I never underestimate a sidewinder."

"I take that as a compliment. And, frankly, were it up to me, we'd have shot you from ambush." Keller frowned at the swarthy killer beside him. "But my associate wanted to confront you face-to-face. He seems to think he'll never be able to hold his head up in public again if he doesn't."

Harvey stood with his legs in a wide stance, his arm poised to draw. As usual, he had nothing to say. He always let his pistol do his talking for him.

Fargo gave the Henry to Cynthia, saying under his breath, "If he beats me, shoot them both before I hit the ground or they'll kill you next." She nodded, and he moved forward until he was five paces from them, close enough to see the burning gleam in Harvey's eyes and the beads of perspiration on Keller's forehead.

"I can still achieve everything I wanted," the latter said. "Once Harvey kills you, I'll hide the strongbox and fall back on my original plan. Prescott and the others will be disposed of, and the Silverlode will be mine. All that valuable ore! All that power! Think of it."

Fargo was thinking that Keller was doing it again, distracting him just as Keller had done the night before when Sheffield's bunch arrived. There had to be a reason, one that wasn't hard for Fargo to guess. Keller was trying to give Harvey an edge.

Fargo focused on the killer's gun hand. When it leaped, so did his. No one could ever say which of the two revolvers boomed first, but it was Harvey, not Fargo, who swayed like a reed in the wind, banged a second shot into the soil, and toppled like a redwood and didn't move.

Just then there was another shot. Fargo looked up.

Luther Keller stood there, having drawn a small pistol from under his jacket. But where his left eye had been was a hole that oozed blood. Astonishment etched his features as he collapsed.

"I told him I wasn't afraid anymore," Percy Porter

proudly declared. In his right hand was his derringer, smoking from the barrel. "But he laughed at me. He didn't believe I could do it. Well, I guess I showed him."

"You sure did," Fargo said.

One deed remained to be done. Astride the Ovaro, Fargo rode up alongside two girls bustling along Silver Flat's main street. "Good afternoon, ladies."

Molly and little Susie smiled in delight. "Mr. Fargo!" Flora's oldest squealed. "You're back! We heard how you saved the mine. Ma says she can't wait to see you again."

Fargo bent down. "I'd like you to give her something for me." He placed an envelope in Molly's hand. "Take it straight home. Promise?"

"Sure, I promise. But come with us. Ma will be cooking supper soon."

"Another time, maybe. Enjoy your ride on the riverboat."

"Huh?"

Skye Fargo touched the older girl's cheek and grinned at Susie. Reining the stallion around, he tapped his spurs and didn't look back until the town had been swallowed by distance and was no more than a brown blot at the base of the emerald foothills.

LOOKING FORWARD!
The following is the opening
section from the next novel in the exciting
Trailsman series from Signet:

THE TRAILSMAN #221
CALIFORNIA CRUSADER

*1860—California, where the word of God falls on
godless ears and where a fast draw and hot lead are the
only sure paths to redemption. . . .*

A feeling of contentment crept over Skye Fargo as he and
his big pinto stallion rode slowly through the tall pine, fir,
and incense cedar trees. He inhaled the balsamic scent of
the forest and was glad the army didn't need his services
again anytime soon. This was beautiful country. He'd seen
it before, but he'd sure like to explore it some more.

Curly fronds of new ferns appeared almost primeval to
his appreciative eye, growing in clumps beneath the trees.
Small yellow and purple flowers poked their heads through
what looked like hundreds of years' worth of fallen leaves
and conifer needles. The thick mulch muted the sound of
the Ovaro's hooves, making the impression of otherworldli-
ness almost palpable.

As if to remind Skye Fargo that he lived on this earth
with the rest of God's creatures, red squirrels scolded him
from tree trunks and birds chirped lustily at one another
from branches. He startled a deer, which turned and bolted
off through the trees. If he didn't know better, he might just

believe himself to be the first human being ever to travel through these woods.

He did know better, however. Indians had lived here for generations, leaving Mother Nature's handiwork pretty much as they'd found it. Then the Spaniards had come and subjugated the Indians, using the land to graze huge herds of cattle. Indians and Spaniards were no longer the only humans living here now, though. Fargo considered that something of a shame.

California. Land of sunshine and gold. Fargo appreciated the sunshine; indeed, he lifted his bearded face and allowed the sun's rays to soak into his skin, and he basked in the heat like a lizard. He wished nobody had ever discovered gold here, because the pristine beauty of this magnificent place wouldn't last long once the white men got to trampling it underfoot. Hell, they already had, in spots. California had been declared a state a scant year after gold was discovered.

He sighed, wishing the white man, in his pursuit of civilization, didn't always cut such a swath of destruction wherever he went. But that was the nature of the beast, he reckoned, and who was he to argue?

A discordant sound smote his ears, and he frowned. If there was one thing that could bring a fellow back to earth with a thump and remind him he wasn't alone on it, it was hearing the racket generated by a human squabble. Who the hell was that, shouting and arguing and spoiling the stillness of the day? He sighed again, heavily. He couldn't seem to get away from trouble, no matter how hard he tried.

Here he'd been thinking he'd make a peaceful visit to Gus Perkins in Barley Flats, as long as he was in California on army business, and not have to deal with anything more difficult than deciding which of Gus's sporting girls to bed. He should have known better. Peace and Skye Fargo didn't often find themselves in the same place at the same time for very long.

He listened awhile longer. The noises were becoming more distinct. "Shoot, there's a woman involved," he muttered to his horse. "And she sounds scared."

The Ovaro jingled the bit as if he were suitably outraged.

He pondered his options. They became fewer when he heard the woman shout, "No! No, you vicious fiend! Stop that!"

"Aw, hell." He frowned and nudged his horse to the right, through a stand of towering fir trees, in the direction of the strife.

Whoever the voices belonged to, they were making such a din that they didn't hear Fargo's approach. When he rode past a clump of mesquite bushes into a clearing, he viewed an interesting spectacle.

Four men, drunk as he'd suspected, surrounded a lone woman. The men were laughing. The woman wasn't. Rather, she was berating the men in no uncertain terms and stamping her foot as if she meant it. Fargo folded his hands over the saddle horn and watched for a moment, entertained. A mule cropped grass at the other end of the clearing. Since it held a sidesaddle and heavily laden saddlebags, Fargo assumed it had been the woman's means of transportation before the contretemps had begun.

"Whooo," slurred one of the men—miners, from the looks of them. "Ain't she a hellcat, though, Pete?"

"Don't you dare swear in my presence, you abandoned wretch!"

The woman, whose face was bright pink with rage, wasn't an altogether bad-looking article—or wouldn't be if she ever calmed down again. Her clothing was kind of prudish, though. She wore a black dress, high-necked and prim. Her hair might be kind of pretty if she didn't have it braided and wrapped up in such an uninviting way. It looked sort of reddish, although that might be a trick of the light filtering through the surrounding trees. Her high-topped shoes were laced to within an inch of their lives. So was she, for that matter. Her bonnet had been snatched by one of the miners, who dangled it by its ribbons between dirty fingers. The woman made occasional grabs for it, but the miner avoided her swipes, staggering backward as he did so, laughing as if he hadn't had such sport in a long time.

"Come on, now, ma'am. We're only playin' with ya a little bit. We don't mean ya no harm."

"No harm?" the woman shrieked. "No *harm*? Why you drunken louts!"

Fargo shook his head when the woman managed to get hold of her bonnet and started a tugging match with the miner who still held the ribbons.

"Listen, lady," another miner said. "We was just relaxin' here in the shade when you come up to us. We didn't do nothin' to you."

"I was *lost*," the woman cried. "I needed *help*! And what did I find? Four men who are lost to all decency!"

"That ain't fair, ma'am," the man said. He seemed the most judicious, if not the most sober, of the four miners. "We didn't expect no lady to interrupt us. We was just havin' ourselves a little celebrash—celebray—party."

"We was happy to help you," said another. "But you started in on us, tellin' us how dishgushtin' we was."

They had a point, if they were speaking the truth. No fellow appreciated being lit into for excessive drinking by an interfering female, and a stranger to boot. Nevertheless, Skye Fargo knew where his duty lay. The woman was crying now. He judged her tears were more from anger than from fright.

He plucked his Colt out of his holster and, thus armed, he urged the Ovaro forward. In order to get everybody's attention, he gave one short sharp whistle through his teeth.

The woman clapped her hands to her ears. The miners, less stable on their pins than she, tried to spin around. Two of them fell over for their efforts.

The one who'd held the bonnet said, "Shoot, who's that?"

The judicious one, from his new position on his butt in the clearing, shook his head to clear it. The other two men only gaped at him, their mouths hanging open, their bleary eyes blinking, as if they were trying to focus them.

"I think you four ought to say you're sorry and clear out of here now. The lady doesn't appreciate your attentions."

The woman dropped her hands from her ears. They immediately formed fists, which she propped on her hips in a belligerent pose. "I should say I don't!"

One of the men moved. Fargo didn't know if the move was voluntary or if it was the whiskey making him sway, but he wasn't taking chances. He cocked the Colt. "Don't try anything."

"I—I ain't doin' nothin'," said the man and he staggered back.

Fargo shook his head and peered at the woman. "I don't think they meant you any real harm, ma'am."

"No?" The woman glared at her former tormenters. One of her hands left its perch on her hip to brush a few strands of hair out of her eyes.

She shook her finger at the four men, who stared at her with varying expressions on their faces, the primary one of which was befuddlement. "Shame on you all. *Shame* on you!"

Not one of the men dared speak in the face of her reproaching finger. She folded the finger up into a fist and propped it on her hip again. "I suppose it was the evil of the devil's brew doing the harm for them," she said scornfully.

Skye Fargo didn't sneer at her. He knew that whiskey did bad things to men when they drank too much of it, but he wouldn't personally stigmatize it as evil, or as coming from the devil. He liked a good snort of bourbon occasionally himself. Because he felt sort of sorry for the woman, he said, "Probably. They don't seem to be really bad fellows."

She sucked in about a bushel of air and let it out gradually. Fargo blinked, because when she did it, he realized she had quite a bosom on her. Too bad she didn't seem like the sort to share it with a lonely traveler.

She eyed the four men and her expression turned sympathetic. "Poor misguided souls."

Although he wouldn't go as far as all that, Fargo said, "Right. So, do you need some help, ma'am? I heard you say you were lost."

One of the miners bobbed his head. "She shed she was losht."

The woman shuddered. "Not as lost as the four of you, I fear."

She went to her mule and flipped open a saddle bag. When she came back, her hands were full of tracts, which she began to distribute to the four men. "Here. When you sober up, I want you to read these. Perhaps this experience was ordained by God to guide you into the light."

"Th'light?" The bonnet-holding miner blinked fuzzily a couple of times.

"The light of Jesus Christ, my good man." The woman's smile could only be described as radiant. "He will lead you from the paths of wickedness and onto the narrow path of righteousness. *He* will guide you away from the lures of liquor and sin. *He* will purify your life!"

Fargo didn't know about those poor fools, but he didn't want to be led away from the lures of liquor and sin. Before she got too wound up, he said, "Uh, ma'am, if you want me to help you get to wherever you're going, maybe we ought to start before the light fades."

One of the miners gave him a grateful smile. "Yeah. Good idear."

The woman didn't appreciate Fargo's interruption. She frowned up at him. "One moment, if you will, sir. These men need my help. They are the reason I'm here." She shook a tract at him.

"We are?" The four men gaped at her.

Since none of the miners seemed to be in the mood for violence, Fargo holstered his Colt, although he didn't drop his guard.

"Indeed you are. I came to California to spread the light." The woman finished handing out her tracts, dusted her hands together, and beamed at the four miners as if she'd done an important day's work. "There. Now I'm going to go to Barley Flats, my dear sirs, and should any one of you feel the need to talk to someone about asking God's divine grace into your heart in order to cleanse your life, please look me up. My name is Miss Genevieve Wiley, and I shall be happy to pray with you."

"P-pray?" One judicious miner goggled.

"Indeed, my good fellow." She clutched her hands together at her waist and got an evangelistic light in her eyes that Fargo feared boded ill for the rest of his trip to Barley Flats. "In fact, I do believe the four of you—" She shot Fargo a glance and decided, with a nod and a smile, to include him. "That is to say, the *five* of you—could use some of God's grace to rain down upon you right this minute."

"Uh, ma'am—"

She held up a hand to forestall Fargo's further comments. "No, my blessed, heaven-sent rescuer—"

"Resh-cuer?" The bonnet-holding miner, who hadn't tried to rise, turned over, cradled his head on his folded arms, and shut his eyes.

The judicious miner muttered, "Heav'n shent?"

"Yes. My gallant, heaven-sent rescuer and the four of

you deserve some prayers." She held her arms up to the heavens, shut her eyes, and started in. "Our precious Heavenly Father, please take these sinners into Your divine care. Lead them away from the path of wickedness, and show them the light of Your blessed mercy."

She looked like she was in some kind of ecstacy. Fargo had usually seen that expression on women's faces under different circumstances. He wondered if it was blasphemous to think of them now.

Miss Wiley paused in her oratory, opened her eyes, and seeing that her audience hadn't even bothered to bow their heads, much less close their eyes prayerfully, she frowned. Fargo hoped she wouldn't lay into them again.

She didn't. Evidently deciding it wasn't worth the energy it would take to penetrate the fuzzy brains of a quartet of drunken miners, she concluded quickly. "Please care for them and keep them in Thy mercy. In the name of your Son, Jesus Christ, Amen."

"Amen," Fargo muttered.

"Amen," mumbled the judicious miner.

"Amen," slurred another one.

The bonnet-holder sent a sonorous snore up to heaven.